THE INVISIBLE MEN

THE INVISIBLE MEN

The Jon Kirk of Ares Chronicles: Book 2

GARY LOVISI

Map of Ares by Lucille Cali

A Scientific Romance inspired by Edgar Rice Burroughs'
John Carter Series and set upon the faraway planet Ares

WILDSIDE PRESS

NAMES OF PEOPLE AND PLACES APPEARING IN THE JON KIRK CHRONICLES

AFTERWORLD: the land of the dead where the spirits of all the deceased of Ares reside.

ANDU: a great warrior and a friend to Jon Kirk.

ARES: the planet under the red sun in the Orion System that Earthman Jon Kirk finds himself transported to through a machine controlled by Tar-gool, and eventually where he becomes Emperor of the Green Empire.

ARESANS: the human-like peoples who are the inhabitants of the planet Ares and the Two continents, Cos and Vognar, of Greens and Blues, respectively. In the eastern lands most of the men are green skinned with dark hair, while the women are lighter in color and have red or green hair. In the western lands the people are blue-skinned with black or white hair.

ARBORAN WILDERNESS: thick jungle-like forest in a secluded northern land of the eastern continent of Ares.

ARMEN: King of the Sar Nomads, and a friend of Jon Kirk.

ARON THE ELDEST: a green man over 800 years old, the leader of the Old Ones of Keva and one of the most powerful men possessing mind powers.

BEDAR: the king of Sfol, a small city-state on Ares.

BEEL: Blue Vognar soldier, who with Corvo under Kevan mind control allows John Kirk, Zaor and Shamar to escape Vognar in a stolen airship.

BLACK DRAGONS, THE: the elite Green Empire bodyguard of Emperor Jon Kirk.

BLUES: common name of the blue-skinned people who live on the western continent of Ares, called Vognar. They are also called Vognars.

BRON: Zaran Winged-man and successor to Grusus, killed in battle by Jon Kirk.

CALAIT: name of the old Zaran city that was renamed Tarcos.

CHAVAS: a rat-like creature, also it is a high insult to be called a *chavas*.

CORON: a farmer and warrior.

CORVO: Blue Vognar soldier, who with Beel under Kevan mind control allows John Kirk, Zaor and Shamar to escape Vognar in a stolen airship.

COS: the eastern continent of the planet Ares inhabited by the green human-like race and until recently controlled by the Winged-men of Zar.

CROOCH: a Southern Farmer and a vile traitor whose treachery knows no bounds.

DAMETON: the brother of Tazo, from the Southern Farmer Caste and a friend to Jon Kirk.

DARG: called "king" of prisoners in the cells before the Games of Zar.

GREEN EMPIRE: new empire created by Jon Kirk comprised of liberated Zaran cities on the continent of Cos with Tarcos as the capitol.

GREENS: common name for the green-skinned people of Ares, most of whom live on the eastern continent of Cos.

GOPON: Zaran, overseer of female slaves in the palace of the King of Caliat.

GURSUS: Winged-man who came from Zar to re-conquer Ares for Zar. A particularly brutal creature, killed by Jon Kirk in battle.

HOAM: an Ares green man general, defeated by the Winged-men in the distant past, known today as Hoam the Hero, and the direct ancestor of the treacherous King Tob.

JON KIRK: Adventurous Earthman and heroic soldier transported to the planet Ares. He becomes the Emperor of the Green Empire of Ares and marries Lady Sirah.

KEN: fleet commander under Lord Admiral Mentep commander of the Grand Fleet of the Vognars during their invasion of the eastern continent of Ares.

KEV: small hidden village on the western continent that some believe may be the home of the remnants of mythical Keva.

KEVA: hidden and mythical secret city on the eastern continent of Cos where the people have tremendous mind powers. Shamar is their king. See Kev.

KONOR: Blue rebel and the new king of the Kingdom of Lanar on the western continent of Ares.

LANAR: a kingdom of the Blues and Greens on the western continent of Vognar on Ares, formerly under the rule of the tyrant Okvon and the blue-skinned Vognars, but now free and ruled under Konor their king.

LANUS: one of the Old Ones of Keva.

LAAR: one of the venerable Old Ones of Keva.

MANALIA: Zaor's mate, green-skinned, fire-red haired women.

MENTEP: Lord Admiral of the Vognar Grand Fleet and leader of the invasion of the eastern continent, also brother of Vognar Supreme Leader Okvon. OGZ: one of the Vaki Nomads, a mighty rival to Armen and his tribe.

OKVON: brutal Supreme Leader of the Blue Vognars of the western continent of Ares.

OLAR: one of the venerable Old Ones of Keva.

OLD ONES: members of the Council of Keva who have special mind powers. Aron The Eldest is their leader.

ON-VAN: military officer who led a mutiny of green warriors in Scresa.

ORLAZ: a madman held prisoner in the cells under the Arena.

ORTON: Zaran prince, new ruler of Caliat after his father, Pondonan is killed by Jon Kirk. He was later also killed by Jon Kirk in a duel.

OXLN: small Ares creature that uses camouflage to make it invisible to its enemies.

PONDONAN: Zaran ruler of Caliat, killed by Jon Kirk. He was the father of Orton, who succeeded him, also killed by Jon Kirk.

POURK: a large reptilian animal used much in the same way as a horse is upon the Earth on the planet Ares. They are very fast moving beasts.

SAHN JOR: King of the Caste of Woodworkers who becomes a great friend to Jon Kirk, and a key administrator of Tarcos and

First Minister of The Green Empire of Ares under Emperor Jon Kirk.

SALIAD: the third and last Winged-man of Zar King of Caliat before the city is conquered. He is killed by Jon Kirk in battle after the Games of Zar.

SCRESA: a city formerly occupied by the Winged-men, now one of the six cities of the Green Empire of Jon Kirk.

SFOL: far off city-state on the eastern continent of Ares ruled by King Bedar.

SHAMAR: the young and heroic king of the secret city of Keva. SIRAH: the green-haired beauty who would become the mate of Earthman, Jon Kirk, and later become Lady Sirah, Empress of Ares. Mother of Alun Kirk.

SAOK: a friend to Jon Kirk and Zaor.

SERPENT WATER: a deadly and dangerous ocean between the two continents of Ares, the eastern continent of Cos and the western continent of Vognar. It is said to be full of sea monsters. In certain small hidden areas it is sometimes shallow enough where it can be crossed on foot or by mounted men.

TAL: a major in Jon Kirk's Black Dragons who leads the battle outside Tarcos.

TAM: Tarcos scout murdered by Zaran leader, Bron.

TARCOS: formerly the Zaran city of Caliat, renamed in honor of Tar-Gool when it was conquered by Jon Kirk.

TAR-GOOL: an ancient green man, patriot and great scientist whose mission was to free his people from the Winged-men, the city Tarcos was later named in his honor.

TAVAN: a Southern Farmer.

TOB. king of the Warrior Caste traitor and enemy of Jon Kirk.

TOR: small city-state on the eastern continent conquered by the Zarans under Grusus.

UNKNOWN LAND: another name for the mysterious western continent of Ares, also called Vognar.

VAAR: Blue Vognar officer who captured Jon Kirk, Zaor and Shamar.

VAKON: a Southern Farmer, a treacherous fiend in league with the vile Crooch.

VOGNAR: the mythical unknown land of western continent of the planet Ares, also the name of the blue-skinned people who live there.

VOGNARS: the Blues, or blue-skinned people who live on the western continent of Ares.

ZAR: the original home planet of the Winged-men, or Zarans.

ZARANS: the name the Winged-men call themselves. They came to Ares ages ago in spaceships from the planet Zar and conquered the planet and its native human-like green hued people, or Greens.

ZAOR: a young green warrior that Jon Kirk meets when in comes to Ares who befriends the Earthman, and the brother of Sirah. He becomes a general in the army of the Green Empire and the head of Emperor Jon Kirk's Black Dragon bodyguard.

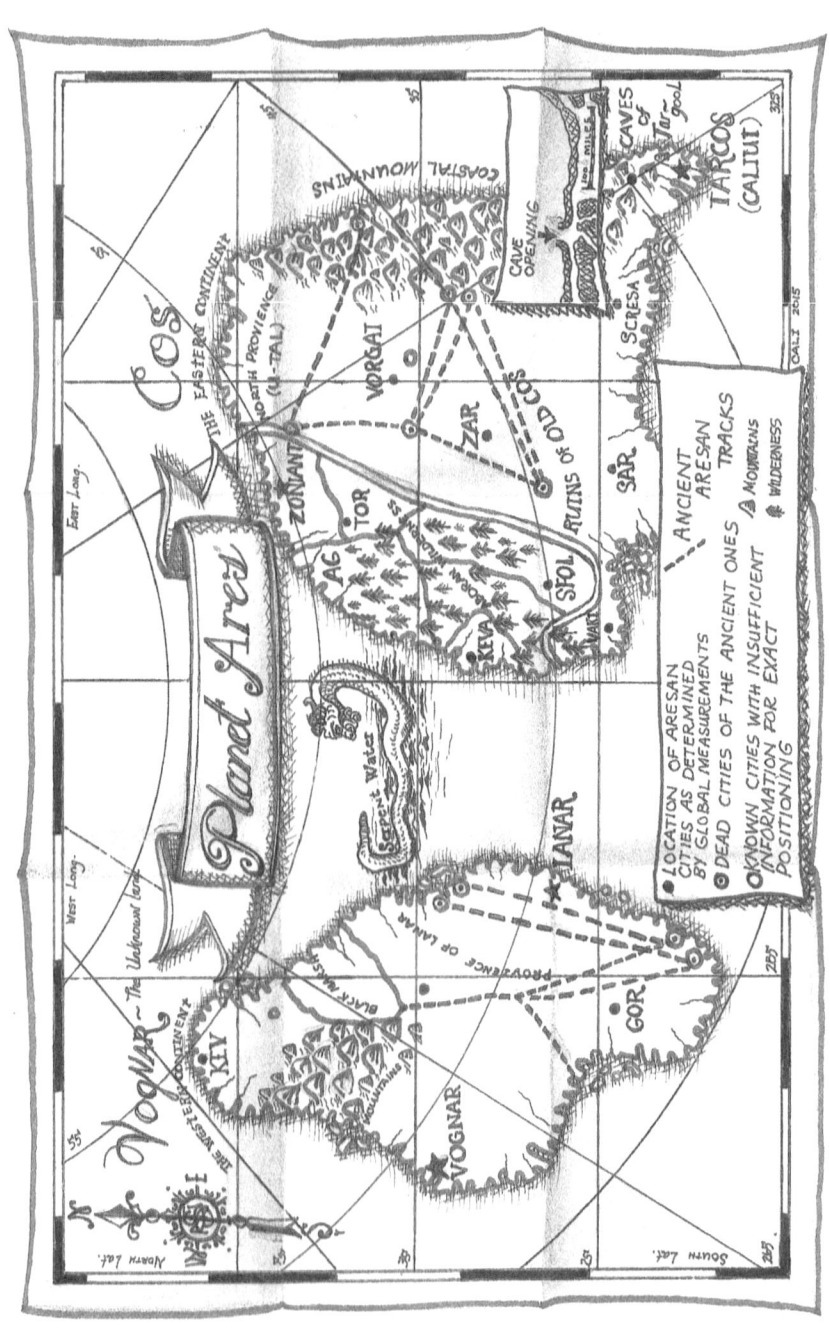

CHAPTER 1

JON KIRK AGAIN!

A year had passed—a long and silent twelve months since I had last heard any word of my friend, Jon Kirk. Jon Kirk who had mysteriously been transported to the wild warlike planet of Ares. His is a very complicated story. Sadly, my childhood friend had been killed in action in Vietnam in the Battle of Hue. I had even buried his body in a local cemetery back here in the States years ago. I wept deeply and thought that was the end of him at the time, but it appears that for a man such as Jon Kirk, death was only the beginning of his strange adventures.

Then one hot summer night one year ago I had the most unexpected visitor. At first I thought it was the image of some ethereal ghost—and in some ways it was—but it was no ghost at all.

It was my friend, Jon Kirk!

Jon Kirk who had seemingly returned from the dead! Well, to say I was absolutely shocked and stunned would not be near the truth of my reaction to seeing him again. He calmly gave me an enigmatic smile and told me that his image was being transported to me through the emptiness of deep space from faraway Ares. It was all due to an ancient machine controlled by the Ares arch mage and master scientist Tar-gool. I hardly knew what to make of it all back then.

So I invited my old friend into my home and we sat together all that long night in rapt conversation as he told me his strange adventures upon the planet Ares. I remember it all now like it had been yesterday. He told me in detail about the mysterious war-like and long-lived green-skinned humans of that barbaric world; the horrid Winged-men of Zar, truly terrible monsters; of his only true love, the beautiful Lady Sirah, who he would make his wife, and so many other heroes and villains. He spoke of his true fast friends;

the great warrior and general, Zaor, who was also Sirah's brother; Sahn Jor; Ar-men and many more who fought side-by-side with him to free the green people of Ares from the cruel yoke of the devilish Winged-men of Zar. Then he told me how he founded a new Green Empire and was crowned the Emperor of Ares, even as a great battle for survival was about to commence to determine whether the green people would really be able to keep their new found freedom.

Then Jon Kirk's image had suddenly flickered out of focus and soon disappeared. I was frantic, but the image was gone. I had not heard from him for some time after that night. Then one day last week I heard from a friend who told me he had been in contact with Jon Kirk! I wondered how and why that was possible but he would not explain, only telling me that Jon had promised him to secrecy. He then told me that Jon was sorry but he would not be visiting me for a while. I was seriously disappointed. My feelings were even a bit hurt by this news. However, my friend next told me that Jon had made it possible for a manuscript of his recent adventures to be made available to me. He said that I should watch my mail box for a package from him in the coming days, and that it would contain a typed manuscript that had been dictated to him over deep space transmission by Jon Kirk himself, to be delivered only to me to read.

Today that package came in the morning mail!

Now I held the package in my hands and hurriedly ripped off the brown paper. My eager fingers trembling with anticipation and wonderment as I opened the package bursting with curiosity at what new adventures might be written on those plain paper pages. Adventures that Jon Kirk would tell me that took place on a mysterious far away world, the planet Ares.

There was a brief preamble note included therein written in Jon's usual terse to-the-point simple style:

> *To my good friend of so many years, here is the manuscript of my next adventure upon the planet Ares, as promised to you one year ago. I have also included a map of the two continents of Ares drawn by an artist from my notes, which I hope you find useful. I must apologize that I am unable to personally visit you this time as I have in the past.*

I can only put it down to the unpredictability of Tar-gool's wondrous machine that seems to be on the fritz again, and the fact that there is so much happening here on Ares at the moment. Things have become very volatile. I hope you do not mind too much me using this manuscript as a replacement for a personal visit. Fear not, I still live! And I still have a story to tell!

Well, I began to read the manuscript with great eagerness, my hands trembling with anticipation as I turned each page. It began with what was an introduction by Jon Kirk himself about his new life upon the planet Ares.

"To all who read these words, I am Jon Kirk, a proud American and Earthman who has been proclaimed Emperor of what we now call the new Green Empire upon the planet Ares—a planet far away in the Orion star system. Today as I transmit these words to you through deep space by way of a special thought machine, I sit upon a fine couch with my lovely wife, the Empress Lady Sirah, in the royal palace of the glorious city of Tarcos. Tarcos is our capital city, it has been rebuilt and attained much of its previous pre-Zar glory, a lovely city which has been lately freed from the Zaran winged monsters.

"It is now a full year since the last of the Zaran occupied cities on Ares was liberated by my army of green warriors. The Greens—or green people of Ares are now free. I have been asked to become emperor of the green-skinned race upon the planet Ares—a position I neither sought nor wanted—but one I realize must be accepted. As such I now have many serious responsibilities that weight heavily upon me. Power does place a heavy weight upon those who do not desire it, but I only serve to lead my people to freedom and to protect my beloved wife, Sirah. Now I have an army to create, cities to rebuild, and an empire to defend after many centuries of persecution and slavery from the Winged-men of Zar. There is so much work to do.

"Freeing the green people of this world—for Ares is a world of green-skinned humans—has proved a long and bloody task. Victory has been sweet but tragic and drenched in blood, though the enemy is finally defeated and on the run. However it troubles me that there are still some groups of winged devils lurking in dark corners of our lands. These seem to be mostly small roving bands of raiders who have so far eluded my imperial patrols, and the warriors of my personal bodyguard, the famed Black Dragons. As Emperor, I have ordered forces out day and night to eradicate the Winged-men menace from Ares, and if that means killing every last one of the flying monsters that we find, then I was ready to do so. As Emperor, I have given the order—death to the Winged-men!

"Still and all it vexed me that there were still many bands of them that had so far eluded capture and justice. These were becoming dangerous as they grew more desperate and hungry. Hungry for the flesh of the Greens— the green-skinned peoples I now rule. They were now my people too. So now I work for the day when these last few bloody monsters can be captured and dealt with. Only then will I feel secure that this new empire I now rule as best I am able for the benefit of the green people of Ares—will grow and prosper. While events seemed to indicate that the winged menace is a thing of the past and that all Winged-men are doomed to eventual extinction, little did I realize that this was but the calm before a mighty storm that would rock the planet Ares and the empire I have founded to its very foundation. Here is how the events of that story came about."

CHAPTER 2

THE WINGED MENACE

Did you ever have the eerie feeling that you were not alone—*when you were alone?*

Did you ever have the feeling that someone was in the room with you—*when you knew there was no one else there?*

Our senses can play tricks on us sometimes, but at other times…mystery prevails.

On Ares, the planet that I now call home, I have encountered many strange peoples, weird menaces and been involved in many furious battles. Nevertheless it was a world made up of wonderful people and a way of life that sang to my warrior's heart. It was my world now. My home.

I also found a woman I dearly loved, the lovely Lady Sirah, my Empress.

This latest narrative of my adventures on an alien world so faraway from Earth—and so different—tells the tale of one of the strangest and most dangerous encounters of them all. It began one year after my first interplanetary adventures chronicled in my earlier report entitled *The Winged-Men.*

This time, my adventures on Ares continue in the city of Tarcos, the capital city of the new Green Empire I have founded. I, Jon Kirk, American and Earthman, have forged an empire through bloody warfare and against the treachery of an implacable foe. As Emperor I take my responsibilities very seriously, for it is a matter of life and death for myself, my beloved Lady Sirah, my friends, Zaor, Sahn Jor and all the other green people of Ares.

This day in my new role as Emperor, I was holding a special meeting with two of my most trusted advisors in a large chamber of my sumptuous apartment in my palace in Tarcos. The three of us sat there silently with dour looks upon our faces, for we were all worried by what we had just learned.

Present were myself; Sahn Jor, my First Minister; and Zaor, my brother-in-law and the commanding General of the Imperial Army, and leader of my elite personal bodyguard, the Black Dragons. Zaor and Sahn Jor sat there silent but grim until I began to speak.

"You both know we are still having trouble with hidden bands of renegade Winged-men," I began carefully, looking from face to face at the two men before me. They were not only high government officials of the empire, they were my good friends and most trusted advisors. Zaor is the first person I met when I came to Ares one year ago. He is a valiant warrior and my best friend on this new world.

Zaor made his thoughts on the matter quite plain to us. He plainly said that he wanted them all hunted down and killed, and I could not argue with him when I thought of all the evil the Zaran monsters had done to the green people of Ares. The things I had seen them do were truly terrible, barbaric, certainly evil.

Sahn Jor counseled more wisely, perhaps. He wondered if there might be some way to come to terms with our defeated enemy. I did not think it was possible, but I was willing to consider the idea. At least I was willing to listen. Zaor, I knew, would hear nothing of it.

I continued, "It is estimated that at least five thousand of the creatures have escaped our dragnet and are now hiding from us in the far off land of Sfol. I have had word that Bedar, the king of Sfol has been trying to route these invaders out of his country but as yet he has not succeeded. Last night the city of Sfol was attacked. This morning I have heard alarming reports that Tor has also been attacked and now been taken over by the Winged-men. These are small cities, weak, with small populations, but how could the enemy mount such an attack and attain such a victory on two of our free cities?"

"This is bad news, indeed," Zaor growled in anger. "I had hoped the threat posed by the winged menace was over and done with since the battle for the continent of Cos last year, but apparently that is not so. In that huge battle our green warriors defeated a force of five times our number of Winged-men in a bloody battle before the very gates of the city of Tarcos. That battle broke the back of the Winged-men of Zar and their military occupation. But apparently it was not the end of their threat. Honestly, I do not understand it."

Sahn Jor nodded knowingly, "These new developments are most perplexing. I believe you must take action soon, My Lord."

I sighed, nodding to Sahn Jor, for I knew that fact already. Then I said, "The thing is these monsters prove to be much more devious and relentless than any of us ever thought they would be. We killed so many of them in battle but there seem to be far too many of them left. The numbers do not add up, something does not seem right. How can there be so many left alive? I don't know what to make of it. I realize that the Winged-men alive now are fighting for their lives, for their very survival, so perhaps powerful resistance is to be expected from them, but I wonder... In any event, it is a bad situation and seems to be growing worse. I know I must address this threat immediately."

"Bad is hardly the word for it, My Emperor," Sahn Jor stated seriously. "Our victory over these winged fiends must be complete for the green people to feel safe and secure in their own cities, in their own homes."

Zaor nodded, adding, "Of course, and I agree, but we should have killed every last one of them when we had the chance. With Tor in their hands, now they have a base they can use against us. If they act quickly, they could use that base to put your fragile empire into complete chaos, Jon Kirk."

"*Our* empire, Zaor," I replied, reminding him with a firm look that we were all in this together. "You and others may have forced me to reluctantly take up the mantle of Emperor after freeing Tarcos, and placed me at the head of our army and nation to fight for our freedom from the Zarans, but we are *all* part of this new Green Empire we have forged together, and we are building it together, my friends. Let us never forget that. What we have done here will echo in eternity."

Zaor nodded, Sahn Jor allowed a thin smile. Both men were totally loyal I knew and they considered themselves my good and fast friends. That feeling was much reciprocated by myself. We had been through much together over the last year, tested and tried in the flames of battle and war. There is truly no better way to test a man's mettle. These were two brave and noble warriors and men I trusted with my very life.

"Then we are in agreement. I will send a powerful force to hunt down these renegades once and for all and crush them." I stated, waiting for their input. "Patrols will scour the countryside, search every hiding place to root them out."

"Definitely, I heartily agree, My Lord!" Zaor responded forcefully, now excited by the prospect of action against our enemy. I could see that my friend wanted to be in charge of such a mission. He might be the perfect commander for such an action, Zaor could be relentless.

I nodded to Zaor, but then looked to see what my other advisor had to say on the matter, the man I considered to be a wise sage, Sahn Jor.

"It would seem to be the best action to take, My Emperor," Sahn Jor added with some reluctance, for he was not a violent man, nor a true warrior by trade, but still he was a brave man when it came to a fight. He sighed softly, "My concern is… I am afraid it will mean another bloodbath. We will lose many of our brave warriors—warriors we can not afford to lose. There may be another way. Perhaps we can try another tack, reason with these remaining enemies, after all they have been defeated and know it now. If we seek negotiations, they may listen to what we offer. Maybe we can come to terms with them?"

"Impossible! They are our sworn enemies, vile creatures with no nobility—they are flesh-hungry cannibals, Sahn Jor! Surely you can see there is no way to deal with them other than with the tip of a very sharp sword," Zaor argued intently. "They all must die! Every last one of them!"

"What terms?" I asked Sahn Jor curious now.

"We can allow them to live, but only in a restricted and guarded zone of land, without any weapons, and no birthing or reproduction will be allowed," Sahn Jor offered. None of us wanted to think of the horrid way the Zarans used green slave women as hosts to reproduce their vile species.

I shook my head dubiously.

Sahn Jor continued, "They may accept that offer—rather than the alternative."

"I like the alternative better," Zaor stated seriously, "a fast death—and they deserve it."

"They do, Zaor is right," I stated without any doubt.

Sahn Jor nodded, then shrugged as if it was of no account to him if every winged monster on the planet Ares ceased to exist immediately, but I knew he was of a more practical mind in such matters. He shrugged once more then got up and made ready to leave my apartments, "I have spoken my thoughts and made my feelings known upon the matter. It is for you to decide, My Emperor. Of course, I will go along with whatever you decide."

"Thank you, Sahn Jor," I said in a soft tone. It was a lot to think about.

Zoar and I did not agree with his idea for negotiations with these monsters, but I knew Sahn Jor had given us his honest thoughts on the matter and I respected him for that. I knew he could be counted on to do what needed to be done when the time came.

Once Sahn Jor had left the room and Zaor and I were alone, he spoke up firmly, "Sahn Jor is a good man, but if we listen to an old woodworker, you will make the wrong decision, Jon Kirk. He is an honorable man, and an able administrator, but perhaps too honest and decent a man for dealing with the likes of our winged enemies. You and I know what they are—none know better than you—and while even one of them lives our people are in danger. You have made the decision and I know it is not an easy one for you, you are not a blood-thirsty man, Jon Kirk."

"No, while it is true I do not like shedding blood for the sake of shedding blood, I am a solider, my friend. On my old world of Earth I was a soldier, and proud of it. I am a solider here on Ares too, though some insist on calling me Emperor."

"You are Emperor, Jon Kirk," Zoar replied firmly. He was serious but he was annoying me by his over-use of my title, and he knew he did so, allowing a tiny grin.

"Anyway, what I am trying to say is that sometimes you have to fight for the things that are important—and the most important thing now is survival. Our survival."

"And regarding those winged monsters survival is the only alternative we have—otherwise it is death. It will mean our extinction," Zaor stated the truth with stark clarity.

"Sahn Jor is a great man who I respect," I continued carefully. "I see his point. If we pursue the war we will have many Greens killed in battle. These are men we need for what I have planned in the future. For we need to build up the army, build up our forces and defenses."

"Yes, I understand. There is another war coming, a bigger war. I know that. We will be ready, Jon Kirk, My Emperor," Zaor said and he looked at me with a smile and a nod of agreement. "You have made your decision then. There is none other that could be made."

"Yes, there is no other decision that I can make under the circumstances. I do not like it, but it must be done."

"I understand, My Emperor. I would like to lead our force against the Zarans."

I nodded my head, "I thought you would, but I don't think I can ever get used to that 'My Emperor' term from you, my friend."

Zaor just laughed in sympathy, "Yes, well, you had better get used to it. You are Emperor now, it is your title and your honor. You are our leader, accept it."

I reluctantly nodded, "I know, all right, my friend, but I am troubled. What of Sahn Jor's suggestion of negotiations? He is a good man, devoted to peace and his ideas are usually sound and wise. He is one of my most important consular's since Tar-gool left us—save for you and my beloved Sirah, of course."

"I agree he may well be a wise man but he is very much mistaken in this situation," Zaor said more forcefully now. "He is no military man, as are we. We are in a military situation with a military problem and a military solution always works best. My Emperor, we know what we must do."

"Yes, of course," I sighed, the decision had already been made by me, but still I hesitated. I just felt it was distasteful to me. What we were planning now would wipe out the Winged-men to the last creature upon the planet Ares. They call such a thing genocide back home on my native Earth, a terrible word for a horrible action, but here on Ares, it just made good sense for the survival of the people I have sworn to protect. Still, wiping out an entire species was a hard decision for me to accept—though I had to remember these winged monsters lived to feast upon human flesh.

I knew the Winged-men. They would never keep any terms of peace, even if they agreed to them. Peace was an idea diametrically opposed to their way of life—to their very existence. I had to remind myself what they really were—they ate the flesh of the green people I loved and I had sworn to protect. There could be no peace with such creatures, negotiations were a waste of time. These grim thoughts nevertheless weighed heavily upon me when my mind was suddenly overcome by a strange feeling. The hairs on the back of my neck suddenly stood up and my eyes stared intently at a corner of the large palace room.

It was weird but something all of a sudden did not seem right.

I saw the color leave Zaor's face now too, and tiny beads of sweat began to drip from his temples and forehead. It was not overly hot in the room. He was sweating nervously. Zaor looked confused, almost haunted, not like him at all. Something was bothering him.

"Zaor?" I asked in a whisper.

He shook his head nervously. Uncomprehendingly. Something was up.

We looked at each other curiously, for now both of us seemed to feel some strange and mysterious presence of unknown origin in the room there with us. It was uncanny, mysterious, nerve-wracking. And it was unseen.

"So you feel it too?" he whispered softly.

I nodded carefully, concern making my nerves jitter.

"What is it?" Zaor whispered, and I could see he was tamping down the nervous feeling growing within him.

"I do not know," I replied in a low whisper, looking around intently but seeing nothing out of the norm. As far as I could see there was no one in that room with us at all. Zaor and I were alone. And yet…

Zaor also looked around carefully, saw nothing untoward, finally he just shrugged, gave out with an awkward laugh, "It is strange. It is almost as if… But no, it can not be. There is no one here, My Emperor."

"I know that. I mean I know there is no one here except you and I," I muttered trying to think this mystery through, but I said it as if I did not believe my own words. "There can not be anyone here. And yet?"

"Yes, and yet?" Zaor asked firmly. I saw that his hand now rested firmly upon the hilt of his sword. "We should be ready for anything."

"We are, but this is impossible. I have the same eerie feeling you do. The feeling that someone or something unknown and unseen is here in this chamber with us," I said this to my friend in a low tone. The room was an enormous palace chamber so there was plenty of space, you could fit two dozen men in there with room left over. My eyes darted around us once again, carefully examining every nook and cranny where anyone might be able to hide, looking intently at all shadows and into dark corners. Could it be some spy, or an assassin? We looked carefully. The chamber was vast, but there was no one in sight.

There was also no sound but our own. My ears strained to hear any sound not made by us, the clanking of weapons or other accoutrements, breathing, footfalls. There was nothing to be heard, and yet, I thought I heard something. It was eerie.

"I have the same strange feeling, My Emperor, I can not understand it," Zaor replied softly, suspicious and nervous. He did not like unseen dangers.

Carefully we checked the entire chamber once again and then the outer windows, ledges, and we opened the thick heavy wooden door to the outer hall. Nothing was amiss and we saw that in the outer hallway my Black Dragons bodyguard still stood quietly at their posts. The men were still on duty, calm, almost bored.

I motioned to Zaor to check with the bodyguards regardless.

Zaor nodded and went through the doorway to my Black Dragons bodyguard posted in the corridor, "Guards, have you seen anyone pass this way?"

"No, commander," the officer said firmly, saluting smartly. "we have seen no one, except of course, His Excellency Sahn Jor, who left the room some time ago. Other than he, we have seen no one enter or leave this room since you and the Emperor first entered."

Zaor nodded but I could see he was still perplexed. These were trusted, hand-picked, battle-hardened men, warriors of my Black Dragons, who would never lie to him or their emperor. If they said they did not see anyone, then they did not see anyone. They could be trusted and they saw nothing amiss. However, I knew that just because they did not see anything wrong, did not mean that nothing was wrong. Of course, I was just naturally suspicious, but the mysterious planet Ares will do that to you. However, perhaps we were just being paranoid?

The thought stuck in my mind. Were Zaor and I just being paranoid? These were troubled times in Tarcos, and upon the planet Ares, so anything was possible. Danger did lurk everywhere. It gave Zaor and myself bitter food for thought day and night.

Zaor looked at me carefully, gritting his teeth in menace. He was disturbed.

"There is nothing amiss, My Lord, and yet I feel…something".

"Something is indeed wrong here," I stated, my hand moving to the hilt of my sword in instant reaction.

"I still feel it, it grows closer, My Emperor. I have looked everywhere but can find nothing, and yet…" Zaor stated nervously in a low voice. He shook his head negatively, for he did not like this spooky turn of events. He was not a believer in the ghosts of the dead, or the return of those from the Afterworld, but something here seemed very wrong. Zaor could feel it like a palpable thing. I know such an unreal feeling stuck in his craw, him being a fighting man and used to hard reality. This feeling smacked of some kind of dark magic, or…

"We are used to enemies we can see, not ghosts and phantoms. Whether they are real, or just figments from the depths of our minds, I like them not," I stated in frustration.

"Jon Kirk, we have checked everywhere. There is nothing. No one here. No spy. No assassin. However, I still have that uncanny feeling in my gut, something here is seriously amiss. We should leave this chamber immediately. I fear it may be haunted…"

I allowed a grim smile at his words, I did not agree with the haunted part of his statement, for I did not believe in ghosts, but I nodded nonetheless. His words made sense. It would be best if we left this room right away. I spoke my next words carefully and in a low whisper, "I know what it is, Zaor. There is someone in this room with us. The room is so large, he could be anywhere and we might never find him."

Zaor nodded, then whispered, "But I do not see anyone."

"That is just it. Nevertheless someone is here, my friend. I am sure of it."

Zaor looked at me carefully, fearful of what my words might mean. Were we just imagining things? The pressure of great power and stress of great responsibility? I could not imagine this to be true for my own psyche—and I knew Zaor well. But could it be true? Were our minds playing tricks on us? For surely no one else could be in that chamber except for Zaor and myself.

I smiled nervously, looked at my friend, and with a light laugh I shrugged it all off, "I am not going mad, my friend. But if I *am* going mad at least I am not alone in that feeling. That is all I need to know."

Zaor nodded and let out with a grim but nervous laugh in response to my bold words. He was about to answer me when I heard a loud resounding *whack* and I turned to see him suddenly collapse to the floor to the right of me.

"Zaor!" I cried out. I was about to run over to help him but stopped myself.

I looked at my friend's prone form in shock and surprise, quickly realizing what had happened and I drew my sword. Now I knew something or someone had to be in that chamber with us. Some unseen force. I waved my sword around me, cutting though the empty air seeking contact with our invisible enemy. There was nothing. I could not tell where he was, the room was big, there was much furniture, he could be hiding anywhere.

"Show yourself!" I growled in frustration, wildly swinging my sword hoping that Providence would allow my blade to strike flesh or bone. "Coward! Show yourself!"

I worried about Zaor but I could not help him now. Now my blade furiously cut into the empty air around us, seeking to make contact with whatever was there. It was most disconcerting, for it could apparently see me clearly enough to stay well out of the way of my blade. Even as I could not see it. It anticipated my every move, my every sword stroke. So I decided to change my tactics. I would make a sword strike that could not be anticipated. I feigned left, then quickly struck right. Suddenly I was astonished when my blade stuck something unseen but definitely solid and firm. I was sure it was living tissue. A body? The intruder? Now that I had a location on my foe I was moving in for the kill, when I suddenly felt a sharp and sudden blow to the back of my head. The last thought I remember was that I may have made a fatal mistake, for there must have been more than one of them. Then I too fell to the floor my mind obscured by unconscious blackness.

* * * *

First Minister Sahn Jor of the Green Empire sat quietly in his own well-appointed chamber for a long time in deep thought. He had mixed feelings at having walked out of the meeting with his Emperor, Jon Kirk, and General Zaor, both of whom were his good friends. Now he decided to go back to the Emperor's chambers and apologize for his dark mood. He walked down the long palace corridor and then neared the door to the emperor's private apartment. He noted the two Black Dragons who stood guard so rigidly at their posts. All seemed proper and correct.

"Is the Emperor still inside with General Zaor?" Sahn Jor asked the guard officer.

"Yes, My Lord," the officer replied, saluting and stepping aside.

Sahn Jor nodded, ordered the guard to open the door and when the guard opened the door for him, he entered the large apartments of the emperor. Immediately Sahn Jor noticed something was wrong. The room was cold, quiet, and empty. Too empty. His Emperor, Jon Kirk, as well as General Zaor, were nowhere to be seen. Sahn Jor stood there astonished for a moment, then called loudly for the guards. As the warriors entered he shouted at them in dark anger, "Where is he! Where is the Emperor?"

The two guards were aghast, totally perplexed at what the First Minister had just told them. They looked around but no one else was to be seen.

The guard officer said, "We saw General Zaor and the Emperor only moments ago, My Lord. I swear it!"

"Did they seem ill or in danger, perhaps troubled?"

"No my Lord, but… They did ask us if we saw anyone in the hallway. Perhaps an intruder? But we told them we saw no one."

"Come with me!" Sahn Jor ordered.

Then Sahn Jor and the guards began a rapid but detailed search throughout the large apartment, going through each and every room. They called out for Jon Kirk and Zaor but there was no reply to their pleas. They were astonished by the absence of the Emperor and General Zaor. First Minister Sahn Jor was positively frantic, for he knew there was some evil treachery afoot.

"Call out the palace guard and alert all the Black Dragons," Sahn Jor ordered the guard officer briskly. "I want a thorough search instituted throughout this entire palace at once!"

"Yes, My Lord!" the guard officer responded quickly and then left to follow his orders.

To the remaining guard Sahn Jor said, "You, go to the Empress Sirah, tell her what has happened and have her come here at once. Be sure to bring more guardsmen with you and make sure the guards protect the Empress. We have intruders in the palace."

"Yes My Lord!" the guard shouted and ran to perform his mission.

Now Sahn Jor stood alone in the empty chamber, the room in this apartment his friend and Emperor, Jon Kirk, often used as his private office. He stood in helpless anger and frustration at what had happened. How could this happen? Then he wondered, what exactly had happened? He wondered about that most carefully and with growing nervousness. Was it a spy or an assassin? It did not seem likely. It seemed to him that the Emperor and General Zaor had just simply disappeared. They were gone. Which was utterly impossible! The room was closed off, with armed guards posted at the door out in the hall who saw, nor heard, nothing unusual. Their word was incontrovertible. Windows were closed and locked, so there had been no entrance from any winged invaders, which was always a fear. It was most perplexing to Sahn Jor and he feared for his two good friends. Where were they? What had happened to them?

Sahn Jor waited for the arrival of the Empress Sirah. He knew she would be frantic at this news and at her wit's end. Lady Manalia as well. General Zaor's wife. But Lady Sirah's welfare was first in Sahn Jor's heart. For it was her husband and brother who were missing. Meanwhile the First Minister tried to figure how two men could just disappear without a trace from the royal palace in Tarcos of all places? How could they disappear from a guarded room without being seen? Sahn Jor feared for his friends Jon Kirk and Zaor, and more so, what would the Green Empire do without Jon Kirk and Zaor to hold things together in the coming battle.

CHAPTER 3

KIDNAPPED

The man had been walking for many hours through the thick Arboran Wilderness, a dense forest in the secluded northern part of the eastern continent of Cos upon Ares. It was like a thick jungle. The great tall fern-like trees and huge shrubs and vines all casting a black shadow over his path. Although it was the middle of the day, to Shamar it now appeared more like dusk because the huge tree branches and overhanging fern leaves effectively blocked out most of the light and heat from the fire red sun of Ares that shone so brightly overhead. Down here on the pathways on the lowly forest floor, it was always dark and shadowy, cold and very, very dangerous. There were always unseen things that attacked hapless travelers, wild animals and other dangers that lay unseen until they flung themselves upon you and their fangs cut deep into your throat.

Shamar stopped suddenly, his ears trying to pick out some distant sounds from overhead. He was a well-trained green warrior, a man of that race of warriors from the far-off secret city of Keva. Keva was a small but proud city state that had managed to remain free and unconquered by the hated Zarans, the Winged-men of the planet Ares who had otherwise dominated the entire world and kept the green people as slaves for generations. Not so with those of Keva. The Kevans were all valiant warriors, and Shamar, their newly installed king was the best of these, however it was not military power or warrior prowess and bravery that kept Keva free. While the noble Shamar fulfilled all the high expectations demanded of a great warrior king by the people of Keva, he was not the true force behind the power of the Kevan people. That was an entirely different and secret power that no one of Keva spoke openly about.

Shamar stood alone with his great sword drawn out and ready. He knew an enemy was near. He was expecting to be attacked any moment by the fierce Zaran Winged-men, so he mouthed a silent prayer to the god of his people as he pictured in his mind the old shrine to that ancient powerful being back home in Keva.

Overhead, though he could not see them yet, he easily recognized the terrible leathery sound of giant flapping wings, a sound that instilled fear in the stoutest of hearts and usually meant violent death or worse. He knew as a warrior lord of the Kevans, if he was not victorious here today against his enemies, he could expect no mercy.

However, it was not like Shamar to hide at the sight of any enemy, so he stood bravely upon a large open patch of ground he had found, boldly waiting in that small clearing upon the forest floor for whatever fate had in store for him as he heard the deadly winged monsters approaching. The dread flapping sound came nearer, it became louder. It was a terrible sound of impending doom and soon Shamar saw them—a group of about a dozen of the weird flying monster men.

The dread Winged-men of Zar.

Although it was dark down here on the forest floor, Shamar could see the creatures clearly now. They appeared human, or at least humanoid, but they were not like the green-skinned people of Ares at all. These winged monsters had leathery skin, were dark and rather more reptilian than human. They had blood red eyes, long claw-like fingers and their most noticeable aspect was the pair of large leathery wings that extended from the back of their shoulders. These wings enabled the creatures to fly and that airborne potential made them a most deadly species. No one knew where the Winged-men, who called themselves Zarans, had came from for certain. However, there were a hundred rumors about them— all of them bad. The creatures did not volunteer any information about themselves either. They looked down upon the green people of Ares with abject superiority and considered the green people as mere "cattle"—and Shamar knew what that term meant. Some said the creatures had come to Ares from another planet long ago that was called Zar. Whatever they were, and wherever they had come from, they were universally hated and feared by the green people of Ares. And there was good reason for this fear and hatred. It had been well-earned through centuries of oppression and far worse.

So as Shamar bravely held his ground with his sword drawn out and ready for action, he could see the winged fiends coming closer. He could see their horrid appearance and evil features now. He bravely held his ground as his terror grew and the blood in his veins turned to ice. For while he was brave and one who never feared battle, nor even fear death—for such is the final journey of every fighting man—he feared becoming the main course at a feast of these winged demons. That he did fear.

The flying men's superior sight had instantly alerted them to the lone green man who was standing so boldly and openly upon the forest ground below them waiting to do battle. Shamar did not try to hide, he did not try to run, and the winged creatures gave off cries of delight and victory as they dived down upon what they now considered easy prey and a most tasty meal.

Terrible sounds of gory anticipation and bloody desires re-sounded throughout the forest by the flying men as they dove down to the lone Kevan. For these Winged-men were hungry after being routed from the green cities they had occupied for centuries, and like all their brothers on the world of Ares, these winged fiends fed only upon human flesh!

CHAPTER 4

THE BLUE ONES

Keva is an isolated and small but lovely little city-state located on the western coast of the continent of Cos on the planet Ares. It is surrounded by the Arboran Wilderness on three sides and by the dread Marshland Waste on the fourth that feeds into the deadly Serpent Water.

One reason Keva has held onto it's independence for so long is because of its vast isolation from all other groups of people on Ares. Even the hated Winged-men of Zar were loath to deal with these isolated and strange green people. They were not like the usual Greens. But there was another reason for the protection of Keva—it was because of the unique and powerful mind powers the Kevan people possessed. Especially the long-lived Old Ones. Because of the mind powers of the Old Ones, Keva's existence was able to be masked and remain unknown to almost all of the green people of the planet, and especially the Zarans. The location of Keva had been kept hidden, effectively masked, and was an absolute secret. That is how the Kevans had been able to maintain their independence and freedom for so long. They jealously guarded their secrets.

And the Kevans liked it that way just fine.

The Winged-men knew about the existence of the secret city of Keva but they had no idea where the small city-state might be located. Over the years they had seeked it out with various expeditions but they always came up empty. Eventually they did not see Keva worth their while to expend valuable time and energy to conquer and enslave. After all, the city would take much hard work to find, and it only held a mere few thousand green people. It was not worth the effort, and the Zaran's were essentially lazy occupiers. These Kevan people, or "cattle" as the Zaran winged monsters called all green people of Ares were just not worth the trouble. The Zarans—once masters of the world of Ares—would rather concentrate their energies on the large cities they ruled so brutally, for these held so much wealth and power and many green slaves. And green slaves made delicious food for these winged demons and were valuable for other reasons as well.

Until recently, the winged monsters had controlled six magnificent old Ares cities originally built long ago by the Ancient Ones of the green race. These had been cities from the glory days of Ares, when the green people had a high civilization of peace and prosperity, before the Winged-men came. The cities had been conquered by the Winged-men long ago when they had first come to the planet thousands of years in the past. Then the green race had a flourishing civilization with glorious cities, but everything changed for the Greens when the Winged-men came to their world. The world was turned upside down when the Greens had been conquered, their cities occupied—their people enslaved. The Winged-men ruled viciously for centuries oppressing the Greens dreadfully.

Then recently everything had changed again on Ares.

Now the world had been turned upside down once more, this time for the Winged-men everything had changed forever. That was because of the advent upon Ares of a single Earthman, a great warrior, by the name of Jon Kirk. It was this Jon Kirk who had freed the green race from the Zarans and then been proclaimed Protector of the Greens and the Emperor of a new Green Empire.

Of course Shamar had heard the tales of war and victory, and like many of his people he did not mourn the defeat nor passing of the occupation of Ares by the dread Winged-men. Shamar was the king of Keva, a true Kevan in heart and soul and a great warrior who was brave, honest and cared about his people and beloved city. As most Kevans, he was not ignorant of the outside world and recent events that had changed that world, but he did not overly concern himself with them. Now he was on his way back home from an unsuccessful hunting trip into the dark Arboran Wilderness when he had been spotted and saw that he would be attacked by a small force of Winged-men. It was a small group of the flying monsters, a troop of wily survivors who had escaped the new emperor's wrath and were now apparently starving, having been exiled into this small corner of the planet to hide.

Shamar could see that his attackers, unlike other winged fiends of the past he remembered, seemed to be a ragged and hungry lot who appeared desperate for food. That was not good for him. That meant that they were seeking to feast upon human flesh, which was exclusively their main food source and he did not want to be their next meal.

Now the winged monsters laughed as they saw the single green man holding his puny sword outward in defense. They drew their own weapons in a mad dive down to the forest floor, each one seeking to be the first to claim the human as his prize—and his next meal.

The Winged-men screamed terribly as they dived down towards the lone green man, as they did so they cursed threats upon the warrior when they saw him stand his ground fierce and boldly awaiting their attack. Who was he to be so brave, they thought? They would show him! The Kevan did not run from the winged fiends as many people did who were so fearful at the mere sight of these terrifying flying beasts. This man, this Kevan, stood his ground defiantly, sword in hand, determined to sell his life dearly. He was brave and noble, a true King of Keva.

Shamar sighed and awaited the inevitable, determined to take as many of the loathsome creatures down into death with him. The Afterworld would soon have a full load of new occupants if he had anything to say about it.

Then suddenly, and to Shamar's utter surprise and astonishment he heard a loud dull hum immediately followed by a mighty blast of bright light. He noticed what seemed to be a mysterious white beam hurl itself upwards at his attackers just as they came down above his head to do battle with him. It was certainly some kind of beam of light, and it shone with a white hot radiance. As it hit the flying creatures they instantly burst into flame, quickly roasted into so many pieces of charred leathery flesh instantly to become black ashes that fell dead down to the ground at his feet.

Shamar was astonished, "What magic is this?"

The Kevan king had never seen the likes of such a thing before. The white beam had hit the creatures full-on and caused them to fall from the sky and land in heaps of charred flesh upon the ground right in front of him. They were all dead. Very seriously dead. All were burned beyond recognition. The smell of burnt flesh was terrible.

The Kevan king quickly looked to see where that mysterious beam had come from but he could not determine its location. He did not see anyone now, and the beam had mysteriously vanished, just as quickly as it had appeared. He could not see or smell anything other than the roasted Zaran flesh, yet Shamar knew that someone or something was out there, and whatever it was, it was most certainly responsible for this wondrous event. Whoever *it* or *they* were, they had saved his life.

"Come out, show yourselves!" Shamar called.

There was no answer to his plea.

Shamar continued, "We are not enemies! I thank you for your help!"

But Shamar's words were met with silence. That was strange. Now he knew something deeper was involved here. Something mysterious.

Shamar knew this not just by the evidence of his own eyes, nor the logic of what he had just witnessed, but furthermore because the Kevans are not an ordinary green-skinned people. They are special. They hold a mighty secret. They can feel the presence of enemies with a separate sense that allows them to 'smell out' enemies or danger. They also have mind powers that can sometimes read thoughts—though it is only the Old Ones who have this power to any serious degree.

Now Shamar's special sense told him that there was something out there that could be extremely hostile and dangerous and it was not Kevan in origin. He also felt it was something a thousand-fold more dangerous than even the dread Winged-men—and he wondered what that could be. The mystery intrigued him and he knew he had to get to the bottom of it.

The Kevan king's mind-powers told him he was surrounded by a powerful unseen presence, and whether it was an enemy or not, he could not yet tell. However, it did seem to want him alive for some reason. And though his eyes could see nothing, his senses told him—his senses *saw* that something was definitely there. He steeled himself and focused his forces. Then he suddenly *saw* it with his mind power, some blurred image of his hidden enemy.

Now his Kevan mind power, more concentrated and strained to the limit, allowed him to see that there was some manner of ship landed upon the ground of the clearing no more than ten yards from him. He could tell from reading the life forces within that vessel that there were about ten mysterious occupants aboard. It was a rather large ship of some kind, but it was entirely invisible. An invisible ship! It was amazing and he knew he had to get to the bottom of this discovery. He also noticed there seemed to be plenty of room inside this mysterious unseen ship for the small amount of crew, and he wondered why.

Sharmar's heart grew cold, fearful, and that fear grew, for his secret senses told him clearly that while these hidden beings had killed his winged enemies, they could still be dangerous and perhaps even something far worse. He could feel an evil force emanating from the vessel. For the first time in his life Shamar knew real fear. Fear was a reaction this Kevan king had not often felt before and he did not like the feeling at all.

Instantly, Shamar looked hard at the direction of the hidden ship and backed away from it carefully, but as he did so his mind *saw* the enemy inside their strange vessel. He could not see all clearly, but he could make out impressions. They appeared human enough to him, but their skin hue seemed to be a dark tinge of blue, not green as were all real people of Ares. Or, at least all people that were now known on Ares! That was most strange. Who were these mysterious unknown, unseen blue people? Shamar could not see them with his eyes, only his mind, and he could not hear them with his ears, but he knew they were there inside their vessel talking and making plans. They were making plans for him!

Shamar unsheathed his sword once again and waited for any attack that might come from these strange intruders, "If that is the way it is to be, so be it!"

The Kevan king stood patiently waiting for these mysterious hidden intruders to reach him, for he knew there was no escape for him from them. They could see him plainly but he could not really see them well at all—and there was also the fact that there were ten of them and only one of him. Shamar was outnumbered but fully prepared to accept the inevitable. Aside from that however, he was most curious about these strange blue-skinned newcomers to his planet of Ares. Allowing this interaction might be the best way to find out more about them. So he waited for them. They seemed to want to communicate with him, or to take him as a prisoner for some reason but they did not seem to seek his death, or so his secret sense told him. Regardless, if they had wanted him dead, they could have used their deadly beam upon him, as they had the Zarans. So he would wait patiently and see what came of it, then make the most of it.

However, Shamar decided he would rather try to reason with them first, before having to resort to any violence. As yet, they had shown him no actual animosity. In fact, had they not killed his winged enemies and actually saved his life? So Shamar decided to wait to see what would come of meeting with these strange Blues—and what he might learn of them. But if it came down to battle, if that is what these mysterious people wanted, then he would fight like fury to prevent his capture by them and take as many of them as he could down into the Afterworld.

Shamar strained his mind-sight to look closer at these blue-skinned intruders to his world. Who were these unknown beings? These Blues? Shamar wondered about them but he could not answer that question yet. He realized with amazement that these beings possessed the secret of invisibility. He could sense their presence but not actually see them—but they were there. He was sure of that. And now he realized they had exited their vessel and were circling around him, so that he would be trapped and not be able to escape.

There were ten of them and he wondered what kind of man or creature they could be? They were not Winged-men at all. That surprised him. And they were not green men either, as far as he could tell, or certainly no manner of green men he had ever encountered before. They were Blues? But what did that mean? What were Blues? They were something totally different and new. He had heard tall tales and rumors passed down from the ancient days about mysterious blue-skinned men who had once lived on Ares in the dim, dark past. But until today he had thought the stories merely myths. Now he tried vainly to remember his long-ago childhood nursery rhymes and stories and see if they could help him put any part of this discovery into some context. All he could recall was that they were very scary stories. Were these Blues those mysterious people known as the Blue Ones?

Shamar felt the intruders moving in closer towards him, tightening the net around him, and finally he knew that regardless of his fighting ability or whatever defense he might put up against these beings, the king of the Kevans, would eventually become their prisoner.

CHAPTER 5

DISAPPEARANCE

When Zaor and I awoke we found ourselves alone in a large dark metal cell. It was more like an animal cage. We were completely enclosed by metal walls on all sides with the only opening being a small circle above us which allowed air for us to breathe and a small amount of light that barely allowed vision in the utter gloom.

Across from me and Zaor we were surprised to suddenly notice that another prisoner lay upon the floor, obviously human, and a green-skinned man. He appeared to be fast asleep, but I motioned to Zaor to be wary for appearances could be deceiving. Who knew what new enemies we might meet in a place like this? When I walked over to the man, he suddenly moved and seeing us—his cell mates—arose and gave us a friendly smile and a hardy greeting.

"Welcome to my prison, friends," the green man said with a grim laugh.

"Welcome, indeed," I said looking him over carefully. He was young, and obviously a warrior, and he also appeared to be a nobleman of some type. He was handsome and rugged, and a fighter by the looks of him. It seemed he had been waiting for us to awake since we had been abducted and thrown into this cell unconscious. He did not appear belligerent at all, and as we were all prisoners here I deemed it wise for us to cooperate and pool our resources to work together to effect an escape. For escape was always uppermost in my mind. Escape and reunion with my beloved Sirah. In the meantime I wondered what had happened to us, just how much time had passed since Zaor and I had been taken from my apartments in Tarcos—and I wondered where we were now.

"So?" the man asked me, "You have both finally regained consciousness. Now tell me who you are? And why are you here?"

"That is a good question, one I might well ask you. Tell me, friend, who might you be?" Zaor countered cautiously. "I think you should be the one answering the questions, after all we were here first. Where are we exactly, and what is going on here?"

"So be it. I, my fellow prisoner friends, am called Shamar. I am king of the tiny but proud city-state of Keva," he said boldly. "Perhaps you have heard of my city?"

"No," Zaor said carefully, dubiously. "I think not."

I also shook my head for I had never heard of the place either.

"That is good," Shamar nodded happily, then he said with a smile, "that is very good that you have never heard of Keva. But not good enough apparently, for someone has obviously heard of Keva, since those who hold us here have expended considerable time and energy to have me tracked down and captured. Hence I am here now as a captive. And now, you two are here captives as well. So tell me, friends, who might you two be?"

Zaor and I introduced ourselves.

"Jon Kirk? Well, now that is interesting," Shamar said softly. "Of course we in Keva have all heard about you and your great deeds."

I nodded curtly, but kept my humility in check.

"And what about me?" Zaor asked his feathers obviously a bit ruffled by not being included in our cell mate's statement.

"You? No, not so much, my friend," Shamar stated flatly and Zaor couldn't help but look a bit deflated. Then the Kevan laughed uproariously and quickly added, "I am just joking, of course! Who has not heard the name of the valiant General Zaor!"

"That's better!" Zaor said nodding with obvious satisfaction approvingly. "Hear that, Jon Kirk."

"The valiant General Zaor!" I repeated with a smile to my companion. "That is certainly true but I think our new friend is playing with us."

"I was. I apologize, my friends," Shamar stated seriously, then he offered a sly grin, "but it was just too much fun for me to resist. The long look on your face was just priceless, General Zaor."

"Plain Zaor is fine with me."

"My friend is a humble man. Though a valiant warrior, he also has a good sense of humor," I stated with a wry grin.

"That is good, Jon Kirk, for we shall need a good sense of humor now, for we are in a most serious and deep mess."

I nodded, knowing the young man spoke truthfully, but wondering exactly what he meant. All I know is that I had a growing fear I might never see my beloved Sirah again. That would never do. I steeled myself and banished all negative thoughts from my mind to concentrate on the task at hand. I was a fighting man. I still lived. With life there is always hope.

As we spoke among ourselves we found out this mysterious Kevan, Shamar, had heard of us of course, but only tangentially for he explained that the Kevan people did not overly concern themselves with the events of the outer world of Ares. I found this rather bizarre. He did tell us he was happy to hear of our war which had caused the defeat of the hated Winged-men.

"It is good the Zarans are defeated, but I am afraid they are not entirely finished. Too many remain in hiding and they are even more dangerous now. I had a brief run-in with them myself lately, until our mysterious captors stepped in and killed them. Killed them most effectively, I might add."

"Yes, they are still a danger," I admitted.

Shamar continued, "I have noticed a severe desperation in them of late, but also an expansion of their activities. Something has them fearful, frantic, and that is an emotion you never see in these winged fiends. They are organizing for something. They are always so overconfident. It is good you have brought war to them and a long-needed defeat, I applaud your victory, I hope it proves to be the first of many."

I nodded acknowledging his words, then asked, "So, Shamar, tell me, where exactly are we? Do you have any idea what or where this place might be?"

Shamar nodded thoughtfully, "Actually I do. I believe we are a airship of some type—almost certainly an invisible airship—and we are being held by the Blues—a blue-skinned race of Ares people who have somehow harnessed the secret of invisibility."

That was certainly a mountain of new information for us to sift through.

Zaor laughed dubiously at that, but his eyes looked around him in our cell suspiciously. "An invisible airship—invisible men! And Blue men at that! It belies imagination!"

"Yes it does, my friend," Shamar stated simply. "However, it is all true, I am certain of it."

"Then we have a very big problem, and it complicates matters for us quite a bit," I said softly, thinking of how Zoar and I had been taken captive—by invisible men! And as my voice quickly died away it was replaced by a deep grim silence as the three of us thought through our problem now so alone in our captivity.

* * * *

Faraway, hidden in the wild lands of Ares, survivors and remnants of the Winged-men army had now come together under a powerful new leader. Grusus, was an imposing winged monster who had just proclaimed himself king of the remnant of the Zaran nation upon the planet Ares. Though he never said where he had come from, some thought he had lately made the trip from ancient Zar itself with a small group of loyal retainers and warriors, or at least that was the rumor. His closest intimates would speak nothing of his origins, nor a word about the strange blue-skinned nobleman who was said to be the ambassador of some new secret ally.

Grusus told all the Zarans that his mission was to take the lost cities back from the Greens, and that these cities had always belonged to the Zarans and would belong to them once again. He was a powerful being, a primal force, full of hate and revenge and he extolled those actions to the Zarans against the Green 'cattle.' He wanted vengeance and he had the support of all the winged monsters in that desire for bloody revenge.

"We will kill them all!" Grusus demanded, and instantly upon his order one thousand green prisoners from the small city of Tor—a city greatly outnumbered which had recently lost their battle with the winged fiends—were now helpless captives of the Winged-men. Grusus called for these green captives to be lined up. They were already bound and stood weaponless and helpless. Now facing each helpless bound Toran prisoner was a lean and hungry winged monster with his sword out, ready for the order from his master, Grusus, to create massive bloody mayhem. They were hungry for food and now food was within their grasp. They would take it!

Grusus suddenly barked out a loud order and instantly one thousand swords lopped off one thousand Toran heads. It was swift and bloody slaughter. Mere butchery. The green heads fell to the ground and Zaran voices rang out with rapid praise and applause, mixed with blood-lust and evil laughter. That laughter was augmented by Grusus and his many officers and minions. Even the mysterious blue-skinned nobleman seemed to enjoy the bloody slaughter.

Of the five thousand winged fighters present that day in the city of Tor, all of them were overjoyed with the blood feast their new king had caused to come to pass for them. Grusus had provided well and proved a good leader. The Winged-men had retaken the city of Tor, the mother city of the Toran people, and the last of the green-skinned prisoners from that city was now dead. Now they would furnish food for the Zaran masters for many days. It was a good victory and would prove a delicious feast.

"Great and Noble Grusus, thanks to you there will be much happy feasting among the flyers tonight," one winged warrior officer said to his king. "It has been too long since we have tasted the sweet flesh of the green-skinned cattle. The warriors are hungry for more such fine feasts of fresh meat."

"They shall have all they can eat," Grusus proclaimed loudly. "Soon all the Greens will know our wrath!"

* * * *

It had been days since Jon Kirk and Zaor's disappearance. Everyone in the palace, and throughout the Green Empire capital city of Tarcos had grown sullen and grey in mood at the news of the mysterious loss of their beloved Emperor, and their gallant General. The grim news had spread throughout the city like a plague.

No one was more saddened by this reality than the lovely Lady Sirah, Jon Kirk's beloved wife and Empress of the Green Empire. She had not only lost her lover, but her husband and her best friend. Jon Kirk was the man she respected most in the world and now he had been taken from her in some mysterious abduction that made absolutely no sense. There seemed no valid reason for it. There had been no ransom demand, nor any news of a show trail or execution—that last part was a blessing, at least. Nevertheless, the event had her and all those in the palace reeling in fear and shock. And too many unanswered questions. The not-knowing was slow torture. She had also lost her beloved brother, Zaor, who had disappeared as mysteriously as had her husband. It was all most strange, as if the very ground had opened up and swallowed the two men.

Lady Sirah prayed both men were not lost to her forever—that they still lived. For Jon Kirk always told her that as long there is life, anything can be possible. But was Jon Kirk even alive? All that remained to Sirah was her hope in the prowess of these two great warriors who always seemed to get themselves out of any dangerous situation as they had in the past. She hoped and preyed both men still lived, for with life anything is truly possible.

First Minister Sahn Jor was perplexed and angry because his search for the Emperor and his general had uncovered absolutely nothing. It was most unusual. Although all evidence seemed to point to the fact that Jon Kirk and Zaor had been abducted, Sahn Jor could not imagine by whom or for what reason. No Winged-men seemed involved in this incident. There was no evidence of them, nor of the treachery by old enemies such as King Tob, Crooch or Vakon. Sahn Jor could not figure it. No note or letter had been left behind indicating any reason for the abduction, nor any demand for a ransom. In fact there been no subsequent contact at all from the captors of the two men. The leader of The Guild of Kidnappers and Assassins had told Sahn Jor that none of their members had been involved in the abduction. He believed the man upon this subject, for his spy network told him the same thing. This entire situation was most perplexing to the always logical and practical Sahn Jor.

The First Minister did not believe it possible that the few ragged hunted remnants of the Winged-men could organize such a venture, nor would they keep silent if they had been the instigators of such an action. They would let the world know of their ghastly act. So Sahn Jor considered other ideas in his vastly roaming thoughts. With his two best friends gone the reins of government had now gone to Empress Sirah—and she had passed the daily duties of administration down to him—for she knew he was a man who could be trusted to get to the truth of what had happened and somehow find a way to bring both men back home alive.

Now First Minister Sahn Jor found himself to be the de facto leader of the Green Empire, an empire that found itself on the edge of hysteria that its popular leader was missing and that some new mysterious menace had seemingly shown itself—stronger and bolder than any previous enemy. Then as if to confirm this, new rumors of a dire massacre at Tor had also reached him and were being spread around the city to devastating effect upon the populace. The common people were full of fear at the rumors of the return of the winged demons under what was said to be a new and even more brutal leader who was nothing more than a butcher. Some of the people had now seemed to have transformed into helpless shivering lambs who were now lost without a shepherd—with the wolf at the door. This was an Earther expression Jon Kirk had told Sahn Jor about once, and it seemed to fit here well. He assumed a wolf was much like a winged demon on the hunt. Sahn Jor would do his best to desperately become that shepherd and hold together the rival factions of Jon Kirk's empire. But he was no Jon Kirk.

And always the question nagged at him. Where was Jon Kirk? And Zaor?

Sahn Jor soon received the vexing news from scouts that a large force of Winged-men had been spotted and was fast approaching the ancient walled city of Scresa. If that newly liberated city of the Greens fell to the winged enemy, then Tarcos could be next. Already citizens were deserting the capital. Sahn Jor knew the small force in Scresa did not have enough men, nor the military expertise to hold the city if under a sustained attack or siege. Nor did Sahn Jor have extra warriors available to send help. He was afraid that desperation would soon enter the minds of the defenders of the city and that a mood of doom and desertion might became the rule and not the exception among the populace and army. He heard that soon what had begun as an orderly withdrawal from that second city of the newly formed Green Empire, rapidly turned into a full-fledged panic, and then route. Fearful news and rumors abounded that the winged devils were back in force and were worse than ever, out for bloody revenge, and that they were feasting upon the green people of Ares even now.

It was not soon after that when more information came to Sahn Jor's ears of a revolt in Scresa. After murdering the imperial governor for what the people felt was his over exuberant defense of the city by drafting all males into the army, a wily officer named On-Van took command. Instead of preparing a strong defense for the city and the people, it was said he was prepared to have his troops leave the city and take as many warriors as he could muster with him. It was thought he would do so soon, leaving the people to fend for themselves.

Sahn Jor could not believe this bad news and was ashamed to hear that army troops had deserted the city and the populace. They would pay for that when the time was right. However, now he had other matters on his mind even more serious.

By the time the Winged-men reached the walled city of Scresa it was practically undefended, there was a small contingent of loyal troops left, accompanied by thousands of helpless old men and women who had been left there to fend for themselves. These people did not stand a chance and when the winged monsters attacked, though they all fought valiantly and as best they could, they were easily cut down or taken captive. They had barely put up any serious opposition, but those that still lived were taken captive. Many others fought and died rather than surrender against their will to their savage attackers. For those that survived as captives, it was feared that soon many of them would become the main dish on the menu at a lavish and bloody Zaran victory feast.

When First Minister Sahn Jor learned the details of the fall of Scresa and the treachery and cowardice of the traitorous officer On-Van, he grew grim and pale with rage. Was there no honor any longer among the officers posted in the far off cities? He immediately put a price on the head of On-Van and any of the deserters who were found with him. They were now listed as wanted men and considered bandits and criminals, in addition to cowardly deserters. However, he did not have the men to spare to search them out and capture them. That would have to wait for later. In the future. If there was a future.

Right now Sahn Jor wondered what would befall the people of Tarcos when the winged menace drew closer to his own beloved city. He shook his head sadly, then rose to his full height and prepared to address the generals and officers who were assembled in the massive audience chamber of the royal palace of Tarcos.

"Nobles and officers of the Green Empire of Ares," he began forcefully, projecting his voice as he had heard Jon Kirk do in important speeches. "I am afraid that the next week will decide whether our Green Empire lives or dies. We are in a dire situation with our noble emperor, Jon Kirk, and heroic general, Zaor, missing and presumed lost. I have no idea where they are, why they were taken, nor if we will ever see them again. This terrible news saddens us all. Pray for them, but pray for us as well, and our beloved city of Tarcos. While we desperately need the leadership of our emperor, we will persevere without him if we must. He would wish us to do so. So we will make our last stronghold here at Tarcos. Let us be brave in the manner of Emperor Jon Kirk and let us fight hard to be victorious!"

Most of those there who heard Sahn Jor's words nodded or cheered, but some others remained silent and skeptical. Too many green leaders did not feel very optimistic or hopeful about the future.

The people of Tarcos and the other cities all throughout the empire created by Jon Kirk were seething with anger at the rumors that came to them of the murders done to the people at Tor, and then days later at Scresa, all by a massive new winged enemy force led by a monster named Grusus. Many people could not believe such depravity and brutality was possible—even by the Zarans. Other people just refused to admit it, since Tarcos was apparently the next target of the enemy and they just refused to face reality.

So most of the people of Tarcos felt that now they were in the crosshairs of a ravenous enemy and they were deeply fearful about what this meant to them and their families. The rumors of massacres by the Zaran Winged-men upon helpless prisoners and innocent civilians were still fresh in all their minds. They knew the enemy would only get bolder with such atrocities—the enemy actually called these blood-baths 'victories'—and that meant an attack would come soon upon the capital, golden Tarcos itself.

The days passed and there was still no word of Jon Kirk or Zaor, and the spirit of the people of Tarcos began to slip. Where was their leader? Where was their valiant general? What had happened to them? What would happen to Tarcos and the people without them?

Lady Sirah kept up a brave front for her people and many say that it was her powerful spirit that held the city together in those dark days, but those that knew her well saw that her valiant heart was broken at the loss of her husband and brother.

Sahn Jor used all his considerable skills as a more than able administrator to step in and improve the defenses of the city, and to keep up morale, even as he withheld no effort to have his two friends found.

And still there was no word about the missing men as more days passed.

With Jon Kirk and Zaor seemingly lost, fear among the populace grew as the scouts reported in that they had discovered a large Winged-men horde now moving towards Tarcos. Sahn Jor eventually had to establish marshal law to stop rioting and looting as the people became desperate with fear at the threat. A steady stream of refugees were leaving the city by day and night in an effort to escape the coming battle and destruction in what they felt was a doomed city—while many more people from the countryside entered the city in panic for refuge behind the city walls. And while Sahn Jor ordered the city gates closed and guarded, people still found ways to escape the city or sneak inside.

However leaving the city was no escape at all from the coming enemy, even though those leaving Tarcos felt they would be safe by not being trapped in the city when the enemy came. That was the worst action for them to take. Once those luckless people found themselves on the wrong side of the city walls and at the mercy of the bloodthirsty enemy—even though they had feared being trapped inside the city when it was attacked—they suddenly realized they had made a tragic mistake. By then, of course, it was too late for them.

Sahn Jor gave orders to dissuade the people from leaving Tarcos, but he had bigger matters on his mind just then. He was determined to lead the fight against the attackers, to defend the city and fight the invaders to the death if need be. He knew his force was weakened without a strong leader like Jon Kirk. For the Emperor was the only man who could hold all the people and all the different factions together in one focused action and concentrated fight. With Jon Kirk and Zaor lost to them, wily Sahn Jor feared the empire might be lost. He desperately wondered which enemy had dealt them all such a grievous blow by taking away their two greatest leaders.

CHAPTER 6

THAT WHICH IS INVISIBLE

Imprisoned somewhere within the ship of our abductors, Shamar, Zaor and I were busy discussing our capture and who or what our mysterious captors might be. That our captors possessed the power of invisibility we were now certain, for our experience and capture had proven that very fact and Shamar had said as much openly. However, we could not fathom the motive of our these strangers, nor how they had been able to achieve the invisibility process.

As yet our jailers had not revealed themselves. Nevertheless, Zaor and I, with the Kevan, joining us, knew our captor's use of invisibility was a fact we recognized as being true and real and a grave danger to us—but also to all our people. That fact filled each one of us with serious concern. It worried us as captives wanting to make our escape, but it also made us extremely wary of this mysterious enemy. They seemed a devious people who had succeeded in a brazen abduction from the very royal palace of the Emperor in the capital city of Tarcos itself. My very own home! What else would they dare to do? Anything it seemed.

Shamar also told me about a strange weapon they had—which seemed to be some kind of a beam gun or ray projector. It was mounted on their ship and it shot a beam of light that they had used to burn the Winged-men out of the sky. Zaor and I naturally found this to be interesting and we vowed that if we ever escaped we would seek out knowledge about this weapon. It would certainly prove useful to defend Tarcos in the future and I believe Shamer knew just what kind of weapon it might be from the way he described its effect on the flying beasts it had killed.

Shamar explained to me what he saw the deadly weapon do to the winged creatures in more detail and I nodded knowingly, it certainly sounded familiar to me. It had cooked them alive. I asked him many questions about this new weapon, and when I was satisfied with his answers, Zaor asked still more questions. This would be a super weapon on Ares and I said as much to Shamar.

"Yes, a deadly weapon that no one can stand against," the Kevan replied.

"It sounds like it is essentially some kind of a laser beam," I told my companions. Then I wondered where beings on this strange world would get their hands upon such advanced weapons technology. It seemed to me like something I had seen years ago in a James Bond spy movie called *Goldfinger*—now that weapon had been an industrial laser. I smiled remembering the scene where Bond was going to be cut in two with the laser—one thing I missed about America and Earth were all the great old books and movies. It was sad there were none such on Ares. Then I shrugged off my previous life revelry, that was a log time ago and far away from here and now. Now I had to concentrate on the present. I nodded, a laser, well it seemed possible. Advanced technology on Earth perhaps, but here on Ares? I wondered if it was not ultra modern technology, but instead very ancient in origin. A laser that could kill the Winged-men and burn them out of the sky was a mighty weapon indeed and it could prove most useful. I was very interested in obtaining such a weapon.

"La-Ser?" Zaor replied curiously, repeating the word I had spoken in the Ares manner, as two distinct syllables, as if it were two words. He wanted an explanation, as any warrior would about such an apparently new super weapon.

"Yes, but the words you spoke are pronounced together—*laser*," I told Zaor and Shamar. "On my world of Earth they have similar weapons but not as deadly as this one seems to be. This weapon must be very much like the one I remember from my old world of Earth, only more advanced and powerful. It is a very dangerous and deadly weapon. I fear our captors using such a weapon coupled with their process to make themselves invisible could make them all-powerful on Ares, maybe even invulnerable!"

Zaor and Shamar nodded grimly at my words. I could see they felt the same way.

So we had much to dwell upon with this dire news as we thought upon these matters and made our plans to escape our incarceration, and then somehow defeat our enemies. We had decided to work together to escape which was good, but I still wanted to know who our captors were and what they wanted with us. That meant I needed to wait until they revealed themselves and their motives. So escape had to be put off for the moment.

By now it had been four days since the mysterious invisible alien ship had left Tarcos with Zaor and I as its captives. Now Zaor, and I, and our new companion, Shamar, king of the Kevans, were all held prisoner inside an invisible vessel in which we had no idea where we were headed, nor for what purpose. We had not seen our captors in all that time of course, since they were apparently invisible beings. Nor had we noticed any indication of their presence. Our captors had never contacted us in any way as yet. It was all incredibly strange. What was their plan? Why had they abducted us? What was going on? With no contact as yet between captives and captors it was impossible to answer any of these vexing questions. However food, water, and air seemed to be dispensed into our cell by some type of automatic system from the round opening high above us, so they were interested in keeping us alive. At least for now. However, the round opening above our cell was too high for us to reach, and much too small for any of us to escape through. So we waited.

Time passed, the days drifted by. The three of us spoke of our homes and families, told each the other tales of fighting the Winged-men and the battles that won the freedom of the green people. A fast friendship began to grow between Zaor and I with the young man from Keva.

Shamar told us that he was only superficially able to read the minds of our captors but he was trying to find out as much as he could. I hardly knew what to make of this but Shamar explained to me the Kevan people had certain mind powers where they could read the thoughts of others. Sometimes. It depended upon the age and experience of the reader. He said he thought he could read some of the thoughts of our captors, but not all, mostly what he got were only impressions.

"What are these impressions telling you?" I asked in wonder.

"Jon Kirk," he said sharply, "they are coming for us now."

* * * *

In the faraway city of Scresa, the winged monster Grusus laughed as he chewed a mouthful of roasted meat off of a charred leg—a human leg—which bare hours before had been part of an innocent green female prisoner. Greedily, he jammed the roasted flesh down his throat. He washed the burnt meat down with a steady stream of harsh burning Zaran beer. Around him, other Zarans, his officers and nobles, likewise enjoyed their grisly flesh feast. A blue-skinned nobleman, an honored guest, sat at the table in a place of honor and looked on amused. He also partook of the feast with gusto.

Grusus suddenly belched with a loud laugh, "These Scresans, they do taste good! They are tender are they not?"

"Yes, My Lord, tender is the very word for them, soft living and no fighting make them quite tasty," answered one of his officers, a terrible brute named Bron, who laughed back with an ugly sneer. The feasters joined in on the laughter as Bron chewed upon the leg of a suitably grilled hunk of human flesh.

"They are fat, but the fat makes them taste all the better," Grusus explained with an evil leer as his tongue licked up the sweet red juices. It was the blood of the last poor victim who was the fodder for tonight's feast. "It is good that we have found that the Greens are useful for something—after all!"

There was wild laughter at this grim joke by the throng of Zarans. They loved to hear and speak such words during their blood feasting.

"'Cattle' can be most useful, My Lord," another officer added, his mouth stuffed with food as he drowned himself with harsh drink.

There was more agreement and wild response to this from the dozens of winged demons in the chamber as they continued to devour their flesh feast. Meanwhile a group of green prisoners and slaves stood by in chains watching all this in silent terror. They could not believe what they were witnessing. Many of them knew some of the poor souls whose charred body parts were being devoured by the enemy right before their eyes. They were horrified by what they saw and terrified that they would be next on the menu.

The leader of the Winged-men enjoyed the fear shown by the cowering green prisoners. Seeing the fear of the Greens was enjoyed by each member of the winged horde as if it were some dinner entertainment specially put on for the enjoyment of these monsters. The leader looked over at the cringing green prisoners and smiled. That smile appearing upon such a barbaric face was a terrible visage to look upon. Women cried out in terror, old men shook with fear.

"The rest of you shall meet your final salvation tomorrow," Grusus promised in a nasty tone of mocking hatred. He and all his horde were enjoying their revenge upon this green cattle who had dared to oppose Zaran rule on this planet. "So shall all our enemies meet a similar fate."

The Winged-men resoundingly cheered their leader.

Grusus burped loudly, and his companions laughed approvingly, it was their typical response to the end of a satisfactory and most delicious meal.

Above the feaster's, in a huge cage in the massive dining hall were imprisoned dozens more captive Scresan Greens. They sat frozen in stark maddening terror as they watched the fate of their family and friends below them, which was now part of the meal of their enemy. It was a horrible fate, and one that Grusus told them would be their own soon enough.

The horde laughed at this grim joke as they devoured more red meat and drank more of the harsh Zaran beer. They were having the best of meals since they had first heard the name Jon Kirk—since that hated outworlder had first come to Ares and messed up everything for them a year ago. Now they felt things would be back to normal under King Grusus.

Grusus suddenly banged on the huge wooden table before him to get everyone's attention. He used a large leg bone—a human leg bone! Debris and congealed blood sprayed among the revelers. Most of them were his warriors, officers and nobles. They laughed with delight at the actions of their leader and cheered his great victories these last few weeks.

"In a few days we will move on to Caliat—the city the green cattle have defiled and renamed, Tarcos," Grusus shouted to his screaming horde. They shouted back approvingly, anticipating more death and destruction—and the sweet taste of the flesh of the Greens.

Grusus allowed himself to enjoy the accolades heaped upon him by his warriors.

The Zarans cheered their leader and he nodded acknowledgement.

Grusus then continued, "Soon Tarcos will fall! Once that happens, this so-called Green Empire will fall with it! Then we of Zar will once again rule and seek our revenge as we have never before imposed our will upon the Greens. I promise you all, that once they are all defeated, I will devour the heart of this self-styled Emperor Jon Kirk myself!"

The Zarans roared their approval at this bold statement, shouting wildly, cheering him on, shouting his name, hitting their swords upon their shields creating a raucous din. Meanwhile the green prisoners watching this all began to feel the tight noose of doom strangling them with ever increasing terror and hopelessness.

As events had occurred, it was lucky for the people of the new Green Empire that Grusus did not yet know about the abduction of Emperor Jon Kirk—nor his imprisonment. If the Zaran had known this, he would have instantly attacked Tarcos to begin his reign of terror over the Greens. Had he known, he would have paid any ransom to buy back Jon Kirk for his own purposes. However, Grusus did not know of Jon Kirk's absence yet, so he waited, preparing his forces carefully to move upon the great city of the Greens and then take it down.

* * * *

Meanwhile, back in Tarcos, even the delay by the enemy in the attack upon the city had taken its toll on those who grew more fearful of the winged enemy day by day. Sahn Jor realized that his control over the populace was slipping away and that troops he had sent out far and wide as scouts were being routed or killed in various skirmishes. No word came back of Jon Kirk or Zaor and the enemy was drawing closer. Some of the green men were deserting their posts and there was the dark rumor of impending mutiny in the air throughout the city. All the various tribes and clans that had once joined together and fought for one man, their Emperor, Jon Kirk, now questioned why Sahn Jor should be in charge. Why him?? Why not someone else? There were many who thought they should now rule. Without Jon Kirk there to lead them and hold them together, many chiefs felt no hope, or no great loyalty to Sahn Jor or any other. They did not have faith in any of the men their absent emperor had placed in charge while he had gone missing. Things were bad and there was even some infighting among the tribe and clan leaders as they jockeyed for power. However, not one man or woman in Tarcos ever entertained the thought that John Kirk might have run away from the city to save himself. Such thoughts about Jon Kirk, and Zaor as well, were impossible to believe.

Nevertheless, this dark mood of fear and disorder caused considerable consternation among the populace of the city, and concern among the regular troops. Only the Black Dragons held firm, standing together in their loyalty to Jon Kirk and the Green Empire. They had taken an oath to serve and they would never break that oath. But others were not so loyal, nor did they hold so firmly against a fearsome enemy. As more days passed, some did ask, where was Jon Kirk? Some even wondered, had their emperor run away? Had Jon Kirk escaped and left them to face the Zarans alone? None of those who knew the emperor ever considered any thoughts such as these valid, but for some of the foreign troops from faraway places, or those who did not know their missing leader, there were many unanswered questions. As the slim days passed by, hope seemed to slip by with them.

Sahn Jor now struggled with his plan to negotiate peace with the Winged-men. He met with Empress Sirah to discuss his thoughts on the matter.

The Empress Sirah listened to her First Minister's word's with care and concern, even dread, for she knew these winged fiends well, but also she felt there might be some faint hope in seeking peace. Could it be possible?

"I do not like it, Sahn Jor," Sirah began firmly. "I do not trust them at all."

"Nor I, My Lady."

Lady Sirah nodded, then added, "But we must do what is best for the people. If we can make a treaty of peace, even for a short time, it may hold the enemy force at bay. That will prevent the deaths of many of our people. I think you should pursue this action and see where it leads, but give up nothing, make no concessions."

"No concessions, My Lady, I understand," he nodded and set ready to do his duty.

Sahn Jor then sent out a scout with a message for the Zaran leader. It was an attempt to try to open negotiations that he hoped might lead to a truce, or even a treaty of peace with the enemy forces. Whatever the result, Sahn Jor wanted to stretch out the negotiations as long as possible, in an effort to buy time for his city. Every day he drew out these negotiations would be a day that saved the lives of his people. He would do what he could to save as many people as possible. Most of these city people were not warriors, many were women or the old, most could not fight. To even ask them to do so would be to doom them to a bloody and brutal death. But to surrender was unthinkable. So he sent a representative under a flag of truce to Scresa to seek out the commander of the Zarans offering a reasonable compromise as a stalling tactic.

That evening his scout had returned to the city and told him he had been given an answer from the Zaran leader, who called himself, King Grusus.

At first, Sahn Jor thought he might be dreaming. Imagining things. His messenger had returned to Tarcos alive, and he said he had spoken to the Zaran leader Grusus. He had given the beast the message, and he stated the enemy leader had actually agreed that there might be a possibility of peace between the two forces. This was good news but it was suspiciously chilling nonetheless.

Sahn Jor prepared to ride out of Tarcos the next day and talk terms for peace if such was at all possible with a Zaran leader. He feared at first that Grusus did not truly want peace—that the Zaran was just playing a wily game allowing that he was more than willing to talk over the matter of peace, while all the time preparing for war. If that was true, then so be it. In any event, he had to make the effort.

Sahn Jor knew the Winged-men had all the advantages now, and while he feared they were just playing for time—in truth so was he as well. So the First Minister took a small detachment of men and rode out onto the Cosian plains to talk with this enemy leader named Grusus, to see if peace was possible. He knew he had to at least make an effort to save his people and city, even at the cost of his own life.

CHAPTER 7

MYSTERIOUS KEVA

In a small building in the secret city of Keva, the Old Ones sat and talked over the troubling problems facing them and their city, one of which was the sudden disappearance of their young king, Shamar. They were concerned because he had suddenly gone missing. They were even more concerned that they could not find him. That was most unusual for their mind powers usually could easily track any person within their range. So obviously Shamar was somewhere out of the realm of their usual mind powers, which was unusual and called for a new and concerted effort by all the Old Ones together. They feared for their young king's safety.

Those of Keva cared little for the other people or cities on the planet Ares. They knew of no other beings aside from the Greens who they stayed away from, and the Winged-men whom they loathed with a blood feud vengeance. As for most of the green people, those of Keva realized that other humans on the planet were as yet still too barbarous for them to make contact with. They were still too warlike. There were also too many of these other green people, too many clans and tribes, and too few Kevans to deal with them. They found themselves severely outnumbered, even among the other Greens, their own kind. Moreover, none of the other Greens had as yet achieved any of the mind powers that those in Keva possessed. These other Greens were looked upon as mere children as far as the Old Ones of Keva were concerned.

Even so, they did keep track of events and some things that had recently happened in the world were proving quite interesting. Those of Keva were taking note.

The Old Ones of course had heard of the defeat of the Zaran Winged-men by an army led by an outworlder by the name of Jon Kirk, and they approved of that outcome. They watched the struggle of the new empire of the green people with interest, and its new emperor, who was said to be from another world and not from Ares at all. That was something that the Old ones found could be interesting, but it seemed improbable.

However, not all Kevans knew this information. It was held as secret knowledge allowed for only the Old Ones and leaders to hold within their hearts and minds. Shamar, though he was the king, had mind powers that were limited, weak, for even though a king he was still very young and not as powerful in this regard as even a single one of the venerated Old Ones. However, while the young of Keva did not possess the worldly wisdom and experience of the Old Ones, he was developing his powers at an astonishing rate. Aron The Eldest was most pleased with the king's progress. He was impressed with the young man's leadership and bravery as well.

Aron The Eldest, was the oldest of the Old Ones of Keva and the most venerated man upon the Great Council. He was a bold man of strong character and vast wisdom that he had attained over many centuries. When he stood up at the meeting of the Great Council all there looked with respect upon his venerable visage eager to hear his words.

Aron stood tall and spoke slowly with great power in his voice, "My friends, we must find Shamar, as well as the two abducted men from Tarcos, this Jon Kirk and his general, named Zaor. I think you will all agree with me that it is in the best interest of Keva to aid these men and to see to it that Tarcos does not fall to the Winged-men horde. Though we do not have enough arms nor men to make a difference in any conventional battle, it is time we used our mind powers to support the green cause. We can meld our minds together which would increase our power and range, and that can make a substantial difference in the outcome of this battle, and in the coming war. To ignore this call and not to help the Greens at this time I am sure will come back to haunt us."

"Sire", another of the Old Ones spoke to Aron, a younger and less senior fellow named Lanus. "We have a new threat that has come to a head in these abductions of Shamar, Kirk and the general named Zaor. This new threat I insist should be our primary concern and they must be dealt with right away. They are a greater danger."

"And what might that be?" Aron asked carefully.

Lanus stood stately, calm, "Blues from the eastern continent of Vognar. They are here now, exploring, most likely for conquest. We must deal with them soon. They have flying ships, heat beams and somehow they have attained the cloak of invisibility. We need to discover the secret of all these weapons. And soon. In doing so, we shall also find Shamar and his companions I am sure, and then they can be released."

"Yes, I agree. I think we are all in agreement with that, Lanus," Aron replied to the group of Old Ones, each of whom sagely nodded their heads in the affirmative.

Of course Aron had known about the coming Blue threat, but he wanted another to bring it up in council—far better the call for action against the Blues come from an opponent of his than from himself. For that would mean bloody war and mass death, and his beloved city of Keva would be in the middle of it. Aron wanted all factions of the Great Council to be behind this war and his playing Lanus had ensured his support. Aron was not only a powerful leader, he was a great politician and he knew people well.

Aron The Eldest sighed, then spoke up loudly, "So it *must* be, so it *shall* be done."

* * * *

I saw the door to my cell suddenly open. I could see no one was there, but Zaor and Shamar each had the feeling that there were invisible beings entering our cell. We stood motionless, waiting. Soon we seemed surrounded by a host of invisible enemies.

Shamar softly told me that he was sure there were five of our captors in the cell with us now. I could see no one of course, other than my two companions, but the invisible men were surely there among us now. Shamar said that we should remain motionless and not try to fight them, they were all well armed and watching us, looking us over carefully. They were feeling secure in their invisibility since they knew we could not see them.

"They are invisible and they believe they are invulnerable," I said softly.

"They may well be," Zaor growled in annoyance.

"We'll see about that!" I whispered to my companions, each nodding knowingly as they knew what I was thinking and prepared for action.

Shamar accepted my plan of action, softly whispering, "I can make out only light images of them, insubstantial blurs, but they are here now among us. It would be unwise to fight them."

I nodded, even though it rankled, it seemed the prudent course at the moment to hold off on an attack.

Zaor had been surprised by Shamar's admission of his apparent mind power knowledge. I was not. Being an Earthman, I had heard all about extra sensory perception, so-called ESP, and other physic phenomena. Yet I was impressed by the fact that Shamar and so many Kevans had this mind power, which they all seemed to take for granted. He just seemed to know things that were impossible for anyone else to know.

"Soon…" Shamar whispered in warning. "Look!"

Suddenly five armed warriors mysteriously appeared in front of us. They just suddenly became visible, now allowing us to see them. I wondered how they did it. They apparently had materialized out of thin air. It was uncanny and eerie. It set us all aback for a moment.

I looked at these men carefully and with great interest. They seemed to be human in every form and feature, apparently human in every way—their only difference being their dark blue skin and dark black or bright white hair. These were obviously fighting men and well armed, and they looked exceedingly dangerous. They were also quite confident in their prowess. They did outnumber us five to three. However, I did not think it such an unfair advantage now that my companions and I could see them clearly. Their visibility might be the death of them, but I thought it better to hold off on any attack or break for freedom until we found out just what we were dealing with here. Who were these mysterious Blues and what was their game? I had to find out.

"I am called Vaar," the golden clothed leader of these blue men said in a deep commanding voice. He had dark blue skin and dark black hair in long braids. He was well armed. "Follow me. Soon we will be in Vognar. Our Supreme Leader wishes to question you for information."

"That is good, Vaar, because I want to question your leader for information as well," I said boldly.

"Hah!" Vaar just laughed. "You are the Jon Kirk?"

"I am Jon Kirk," I replied.

"The off-worlder?"

"Yes."

Vaar looked at me curiously, then motioned us to move out.

"Your leader will learn nothing from us," Zaor growled boldly, defiant. I could see he was ready for action.

Vaar shrugged and just motioned us out of the cell, "We shall see."

I signaled once more for Zaor to hold off on any attack for the moment. I needed to find out more information about these mysterious Blues before I acted.

Our hands were bound and more guards joined Vaar and his men. We were then quickly marched out of the invisible ship. That ship suddenly became visible to show us a massive airship of some type well suited for war, bristling with barrels for some type of gun or canon.

We were led away from the ship, across an open flat area and soon we found ourselves entering a large city. It was the capital city of the Vognar Empire, the land of the much feared Invisible men. Here we were taken through the streets to another impressive building that appeared to be some kind of palace, and we were locked away in another prison cell down inside the bowels of the building.

Once we were locked in our new cell and our guards had left, Shamar, spoke up, "We are in the hands of a very dangerous group of people. These are people I have never encountered before, but I had heard tales of their existence. They are Blues, also called the Vognars and I am sure now that we have been taken to a strange continent far off to the west of Cos. These Blues may prove to be more dangerous than our hated enemy the Winged-men."

"What do you mean?" Zaor asked curiosity getting the better of him. "Tell us about these people. Everything you know. Who exactly are they?"

"We have been taken to the mysterious western continent of Ares, the continent west of Cos, known as Vognar, named after the blue-skinned race who dwell here. These blue peoples of Vognar— Vognars—or Blues, as they are sometimes called—are strange to me and most Kevans, but there is rumor of them in the ancient histories," he continued thoughtfully, shaking his head back and forth to indicate he was troubled. "From what contact I have had with

Vaar's mind, I can see these blue people are very warlike and violent, and it seems they intend to invade the eastern continent and enslave all the green people there. They are a vicious and deadly people and are ruled by a monster in human form."

Zaor laughed defensively, "They could never defeat all the Greens, and they could never control all of Ares."

"I wouldn't bet on that," I replied with a curt nod of my head at Shamar. "With their laser weapons, invisibility and those airships they might just be able to do anything they want to do. Unless we stop them."

* * * *

Sahn Jor left the city of Tarcos with a small party of warrior honor guards to meet with King Grusus and the Winged-men on the open plain before the city of Scresa. He was of a mixed mind to make terms for peace with these savage brutes—but he knew that peace is made only by talking with your enemy. He was brave enough to make a try for peace. It wasn't easy or pleasant for the green man to do this, or for him to meet with his hated enemy, but he felt he had to take the chance and do what he could for the innocent and helpless people under his control. If he could buy them some time, it might be worth it.

Sahn Jor knew that if a strong leader like Jon Kirk were here, he was sure he would have some great plan ready that would defeat the enemy, but Sahn Jor was no Jon Kirk. He was just an administrator and not any kind of great warrior or general. He had to come up with some plan that he hoped would work to save the city and his people. He knew he had to do something to save the green people of Tarcos.

It came as a stunning surprise to Shan Jor that the talks actually began, and more surprising because the winged monster Grusus seemed unnaturally respectful and even somewhat understanding in their preliminary discussions. The Zaran spoke respectfully and with some decency—at least for a Zaran. This reaction was even more of a shock to Sahn Jor than if the winged monster had just murdered him outright—which the green man had considered could be an actual outcome when one met with any Zaran. But such was not the case this time, and no threats were offered. He was certainly perplexed, astounded, perhaps even hopeful now. It was all most strange.

Sahn Jor wondered just what game this winged creature was playing—or was he playing a game? The winged leader proclaimed he just wanted peace and even seemed to take the green man Shan Jor into his confidence about how important he felt peace was to both races. It was most unusual. The green man remained suspicious of course, for he had heard terrible rumors, but he had not yet had confirmation of the atrocities done by Grusus to the people at Tor and Scresa. Of course, he had not seen any of the results, nor heard evidence from any survivors. That was because there were no survivors, and he never saw any prisoners. With hope upon the horizon he almost refused to believe the wild rumors of war and atrocity. He hoped those rumors proved to be just rumors, and nothing more. But his inner voice told him the rumors must be true. That meant he knew he had to ask Grusus about them—and that might mean trouble. Even battle. But he had to make the attempt to learn all the facts. Although he hated the Zarans, if he could bring peace to Tarcos by dealing with their leader, Sahn Jor would do so. He would deal with all the devils in the Afterworld themselves to bring peace and save the people of Tarcos.

The more Sahn Jor and the Zaran talked together, the more Grusus tried to put Sahn Jor at ease. The Zaran even reluctantly admitted to some massacres by his troops, when the subject was brought up by Sahn Jor most delicately. The Zaran leader did not deny them as Sahn Jor thought he surely would. He did not become enraged. Instead, the Zaran told the green man in all seeming candor how his warriors had slipped his rein, done the deed without his orders. He said he even regretted the blood-letting. He told the green man such violence had been useless and stupid and had been done without his permission. Furthermore he told Sahn Jor that the Zarans who had done the killings had been punished and were now dead. While Grusus admitted it was well known that Zarans ate human flesh—and that his warriors were in fact hungry for food—he said he had ordered his warriors to feed only from local animal stock—and *not* the green people.

Sahn Jor hardly knew how to react to this admission, but he still did not believe the Zarans, for it seemed something was not right here. However, if he could broker a peace that saved Tarcos from attack, then it might all be worth it. He felt he could overlook much if peace were the result. He knew he would have to overlook much and the realization made him sick. He knew Jon Kirk would never accept such a situation, but he was not Jon Kirk—and Jon Kirk was not here to lead him.

"It is much for me to consider," Sahn Jor stated carefully to the winged leader, thinking of the murdered green people of Tor and Scresa. However, it did seem that Grusus was willing to come to some kind of deal. It was uncanny.

"You have to believe me when I tell you I did not order these actions against your Greens, I am regretful at this situation," Grusus told Sahn Jor, who had never even contemplated the thought of a Zaran apologizing to a green man, but this came close enough. "The entire situation saddens me because it was unnecessary."

"I appreciate your candor, Lord Grusus," Sahn Jor replied carefully.

The large Winged-man nodded his head and flapped his large leathery wings in acknowledgement.

Sahn Jor and his small group of advisers hardly knew what to say or how to react to this information when they met later to talk things over. They had never heard the likes of such words before from any Winged-man, much less one of the enemy leaders. Of course it could all be a ruse or lie—and it probably was—but what if it were not? Perhaps there could be a new era of understanding between these two races? If so, should not Sahn Jor try to make it happen? So the talks continued and negotiations began. As the talks continued a peace plan was eventually arranged and finally a treaty was drawn up.

Three days later a treaty of peace was signed. All in all, for a time Sahn Jor was overjoyed that he had brought peace to the city of Tarcos. The terms of peace were that while the Winged-men would spare Tarcos from any attack, they would not withdraw from imperial territory claimed by the Green Empire. At least not yet. The entire affair left all uneasy with the details. For when were the Winged-men leaving? Where were they to go? At least for now the people of Tarcos had been spared and felt safe, they had been saved from the winged monsters for the moment, even though the monsters had not withdrawn from around the city as the treaty had stipulated. Sahn Jor could still see the huge enemy camp just beyond the horizon. Silent. Waiting? Waiting for what? There was peace for now, but it seemed to be a stalemate that could blow up at any time. Sahn Jor never trusting of the enemy, wondered just what the enemy plan might be. He sent out spies and scouts to see what could be found out. Many were never seen again.

* * * *

Venerable Aron The Eldest, once again spoke to the Kevan Council of Old Ones, "Plans are now set in motion to find our king, Shamar, as well as this Jon Kirk and General Zaor, and then bring them to us. By melding our minds our enhanced vision allows us to see much farther than we have ever seen before, and now we will find out where they have been taken. It is far away. I am sure we will reach them soon. Meanwhile, the new Zaran leader, Grusus, seems to have eased his hunger for empire and revenge for the moment. He has entered into terms of peace with the First Minister of Tarcos, Sahn Jor. It is peace of a kind, but knowing our enemy, I fear it is peace only for the moment, and ill begotten. However, today Tarcos is safe, so that is a positive development."

"What are we to do about the advancing Blues, Aron?" Lanus asked thoughtfully.

"Under normal circumstances we would not interfere deeper without dire consequences drawing attention to ourselves, but I fear we have no choice. While we of Keva can not afford to antagonize these blue-skinned Vognars without serious repercussions against our own small and defenseless city, we can not allow them to conquer the land of the Greens. In short, we must attempt to bring down these Vognars and their allies the Winged-men, but we can not do it alone. We need a united strong empire of the Greens to help us—and that means Jon Kirk must be set free to unite the green people and lead that fight."

* * * *

Later that day the Old Ones of Keva grew silent, sitting in a circle of psychic resonance, their minds melding together in deep thought. The manner in which they increased their mind power was exponential and allowed them to enter minds far away and in some manner, to control those minds.

The minds of the Old Ones were now ranging far and wide, across the dark dread Serpent Water to the unknown land of the Vognars far to the west. It was the homeland of the mysterious Blue people, who had been able to tap some of the ancient Ares knowledge that had been lost to those of the present day. Now they had created ships that flew through the sky and controlled the power to make themselves invisible.

Aron The Eldest spoke up, "My brothers, do you see what I see in their minds?"

The One Ones nodded grimly in agreement. They saw war and bloody murder coming to all of Ares if these Blues had their way. If this So-called Supreme Leader Okvon was victorious he would not rest until he found and destroyed Keva.

Aron stood tall and fierce, "Now you know what I know. We have no choice and we must act, and we must do so soon. We are running out of time."

All of the Old Ones nodded once more in agreement, even dire and argumentative Lanus. All of the leaders there knew there was no choice for Keva now and they must join in the war and use their mind powers to bring about victory for the Greens. Or die trying.

"So it is decided?" Aron The Eldest asked, looking at each of the Old Ones for their thoughts.

"So it is decided," each man answered back as if one voice.

CHAPTER 8

VOGNAR

Vognar, was a drab unimposing city of high brown and gray brick buildings. Dark and grim like it's people. There was no color, no joy, the people seemed as drab and unhappy as the city itself appeared to me and my two companions. Zaor and Shamar did not like the mood of the place at all.

Now that we had been taken and locked away in the palace in a prison cell, Shamar the Kevan, was voicing his views.

"Jon Kirk, at first I believed that somehow the Voganrs' blue-tinged skin coloring was what enabled them to attain their invisibility. That is not true. If you look upon their belt, each one has a small device and that is the secret to their invisibility. They can control it, they can turn it on or off at will by the flick of a switch. It seems they have adapted a similar device, though far larger, in making their ships and much of their city also invisible whenever they want to do so, or need to. Once I learn their secret, we of Keva will be able to copy it. The secret is deeply locked within the minds of certain of their scientific leaders, but for us of Keva, that mind vault while closed is not inaccessible. I am sure there is some way to get at that secret, and I know the Old Ones will not rest until they seek it out."

"You and your people must keep trying," I told Shamar. "We need that knowledge to defend against them and to defeat them."

The Kevan nodded, adding a bit of a shrug, "The trouble is, my mind powers are not always a certainty. There are limits. Only on the inside of the ships and buildings can my vision work properly and see what is truly there. I am young and not as experienced as the Old Ones of the Great Council. In truth I have rather weak mind powers."

"What of their invisibility? How does it work?" I asked.

"I have thought on this question, Jon Kirk. It occurs to me the Blues invisibility works much in the manner as the *Oxln*, which is a tiny Ares animal which changes color to match its surroundings—only the Blues device takes that camouflage principle much farther—to complete invisibility."

I nodded it made sense, I had heard of similar situations back on Earth.

"Shamar, how is it you know so much about these mysterious people?" Zaor asked, perplexed by the Kevan's apparent vast knowledge. He had never even considered the existence of such strange people as the Blues, or their home being upon a totally separate and undiscovered continent upon Ares. "I have never encountered people such as these before, nor have I heard of their likes from any green people I have had contact with. How can they be?"

Shamar nodded, "Not all that is known, is seen, my friend."

Zaor looked at the Kevan perplexed by his answer, then he smiled and nodded.

"Can you actually read their minds?" I asked our friend the more important question. I took a guess at what might be the truth behind Shamar's knowledge of the Vognars but I wanted to be certain.

"No, not exactly. I can only see inside their minds at very rare times, but even then it is often difficult to know exactly what I am viewing. Mind vision is not as clear as you might think, Jon Kirk," Shamar carefully replied looking at Zaor and myself—one of us a green Cosian, the other a mysterious white-skinned warrior who said he had come from the outworld planet of Earth.

The man from Keva continued, "I do know what they are thinking most of the time, because they also put their thoughts on guard. My people—the Kevans, who you tell me neither of you men had ever heard of—have been perfecting our mind powers for generations. The Old Ones of our city are much more skillful in this power than I am and they possess it to a far greater degree. Some of them, such as Aron, have centuries of experience in the mind arts. I am sure they are working on discovering all the Vognar secrets now. Then they will take that knowledge and put it to good use for our side."

"I hope so," I stated simply, adding, "I also have never heard of your country."

"Nor I of your own, until you told me of this Am-Racan, and Ea-Arth," Shamar replied with a wry grin. "Our Old Ones—our leaders—discourage contact with the outside world. That is the reason the Winged-men of Zar have never conquered us, they barely know of our existence and have no idea of the location of our city. They surmise we must be somewhere in the north, of course, hiding from them, but they have never been able to discover the actual location. Our Old Ones have ways to numb and confuse the thoughts of those of Zar should they ever come too close to Keva. So the enemy have never found our city. To all outsiders it is lost in the shadows, obscured and unseen by all as our Old Ones stand guard. The Winged-men have never conquered our people. It is a source of pride with us that we remain free when we see the terror they have done to the other green people of this world. We have seen much, but we have not been unmoved by the plight of these people. We have wanted to help ever since the winged pestilence came to Ares but we are a small city, only a few thousand people in all, realistically our warriors would have no effect in any fight. But now, Jon Kirk you are here. You have united the people and created the Green Empire and defeated the Winged-men in battle after battle. Now we feel it is time for us to act. Now the Vognars are involved as well, so we of Keva know it is our time and that we *must* act, for our own safety as well as your own."

Zaor nodded at that grim truth, "It is good to have your people on our side."

I thought deeply upon what Shamar had told us and it gave me a fearful dark moment. These Blues and the Winged-men—allies! That was the worse that could happen. There was much to be done, the situation was complicated and extremely dangerous. I thought that defeating the Winged-men last year had been a miracle and a major victory that ended the war, but now I saw that the green people of Ares were still locked in a vicious struggle with an implacable foe and the war would go on for much longer. These facts were a lot to digest.

We three sat in a circle upon the floor of our cell discussing the possibility of escape. Making our plans. There seemed to be very few viable alternatives.

* * * *

Much time passed. What seemed hours or maybe even days later, a dozen burly guards unlocked the door and entered our prison chamber. With sword points put meaningfully to our backs, they rousted us to our feet and ordered us to follow them. Since they were in their own city, they must have felt secure so they did not use their invisibility here. We could see the men clearly.

The guard commander was Vaar, once again, the same Vognar who had first captured us and brought us to this city of the blue people. The Blues were now visible to us, and that enabled me to take a particular interest in their war belts and harnesses, and at the small box-like device each warrior had attached on his belt. If need be, I was sure I would be able to 'borrow' one of these devices, but for now, I would do nothing and go along with their game to see what they had in store for us.

I looked over at Shamar, then at the small box on Vaar's belt, the Kevan nodded in acknowledgement—yes, that was the invisibility device.

"Come now! Quickly!" Vaar ordered us gruffly. He and his men pricked us with their sword points with deadly menace to get us moving. "You are to be brought before our Supreme Leader, the Noble Okvon. Come with us now!"

I nodded to my companions. This might be the time that we discovered some of the answers to our many questions, or it might be a good time to make our move to freedom. I whispered such words to my companions who only nodded in reply, wary and ready for my command. I asked them to be ready, but hold off for now. We would go with our captors, I wanted to see what this Okvon had to say.

Flanked by armed guards we were led down a large corridor which was dark and drab like the rest of the Vognar buildings. Such decorations as there were on display in the halls, were depressing and cold. These seemed a grim and joyless people.

My two companions and I were then led up stairs and then up ramps through more corridors and eventually into a huge hall, at the end of which opened into an enormous audience chamber. We assumed we were to be brought before the Vognar leader but the huge chamber appeared to be entirely empty. It seemed the

Voganrs were not very punctual when it came to time schedules. Vaar had moved us quickly so I assumed the Vognar leader wanted us to be brought before him as soon as possible. When we saw no one was there and the chamber was empty it seemed strange. But it did not matter to me. So be it.

We were brought forward under tight guard. I looked at my guards and their leader, the officer, Vaar.

"Vaar, why have we been abducted?" I demanded of the Blue officer right away. "There is no hostility between the green and blue people. We are not enemies."

Vaar only shook his head, then finally explained, "Originally, we were sent out with orders to collect the three Greens who would give our invading army the most trouble; Jon Kirk, and General Zaor, whose absence we were told would doom your people and city to easy conquest."

"Told by who?" I asked Vaar. The Vognar only gave me a sly smile but he did not answer that question, then he did continue talking. So I continued listening.

"A month ago our scouts captured a dozen Greens and brought them here to gather information. Our Supreme Leader learned much valuable information from them. Some died in torture refusing to give up any information, but there were others who more than willing to gave up any information we requested. In fact, three of them proved to be so cooperative we have set them free, and they have even asked to join our forces. For their assistance they have been well rewarded."

"They are traitors! They deserve death! What are their names!" I growled, wanting to know who these three dogs might be. I demanded Vaar tell me, intently repeating my demand of who these three Greens might be. I wanted their names, but Vaar only laughed at me and would not tell me anything about them.

I blurted out, "Are their names Tob, Crooch and Vakon?"

Vaar only laughed at this. "I am not required to answer your questions! Who do you think you are?"

I shot Vaar a hard look and he seemed to shrink a bit under my withering gaze. However, the Vognar did continue with his story, telling us, "Regardless of their names, these three new friends told us all we needed to know to conquer the eastern continent—especially the fact that there were two men who would unite defiance against us. We were given the names of two men who were held in such great respect and honor—men the Greens would follow even into the Afterworld—the name of Jon Kirk the emperor, and Zaor the general. So I was sent to find you and take you both as prisoners. It was so easy for us to do using our invisible flying ships and our invisible warriors. Without you two to unite the empire of the Greens we were told it will eventually break apart into dozens of petty tribes and clans and thus be easy prey for our army. Even now, our allies, the Zaran Winged-men, are at the very gates of the city of Tarcos and have it under siege."

I shot a quick look at the warrior in fear. Tarcos under siege? If true, I had now learned something that sent ice through my veins. My fears for the worst that could happen were true, and yet, if the city were still under siege, then at least it might not have fallen. Not yet. Tarcos may still hold out for some time. So I prayed the city had not yet fallen. Then perhaps Sirah was still safe—for now—at least. Perhaps? It was grim news that weighed heavily upon my thoughts. So now I understood why Zaor and I were here. I looked over at Vaar and held down my anger for the moment. There would be plenty of time for action and blood-letting upon our enemy, but now was not the time. I took a deep breath and a moment to regain my composure.

"I understand what you have told us about Zaor and myself, Vaar, but why is this man from Keva, here?" I asked, looking over at Shamar curiously.

Vaar just shrugged, then added, "It is because we realize that by being a Kevan king, he is an important leader from that mysterious city, whose inhabitants have certain mind powers. Our Supreme Leader is convinced that those of Keva have discovered a mind force which can be an impediment to our plans of conquest. So we must bring these Kevans to heel. This one shall tell us all he knows about that city and his people."

"That is what you think!" Shamar barked out with a grim smile. "You Blues seek information from us all for your conquest. You will gain nothing from me."

"Nor me either!" Zaor growled defiantly.

Shamar added hotly, "You Blues desperately want to know how to use our Kevan mind powers. Well, you will never find out what we know, but I know you will try anything to make me tell you what you want to know. You can try all you want, but you will learn nothing from me!"

"Oh, you will tell us," Vaar promised with dark menace. "We have the most excellent practitioners who can loosen anyone's tongue, each well-versed in every aspect of torture."

"I'm sure you do," I blurted angrily at this admission.

"We will rather die than tell you anything," Zaor stated firmly.

"Then you shall die," Vaar replied coldly.

"I am a Kevan king!" Shamar stated with great pride. Then he spit and turned his face away from our captor. "You will learn nothing from me!"

"Oh, you are very much mistaken, you will tell us all we want to know by the time the torturers get through with you," Vaar promised hotly. "Then you will beg us to listen to all the deepest secrets that you possess, you will beg us to listen to them all."

"You and your masters will rue the day you ever captured a Kevan king! Why, I could kill you all now with one simple mind blast!"

I shook my head, telling the Kevan to take care in his fiery words and threats.

"Jon Kirk, they seek to learn the truth of my powers and if there be any more warriors such as I. I should kill them all now," Shamar laughed boldly, his eyes fixed defiantly upon Vaar's nervous face. "They want to know the location of our city, and how many Kevans live there. They want to use our powers against us and all of the Greens. Then they will capture or kill us all. They see us as a threat to their dominance over the world—and they are correct!"

Vaar looked worried. "You are a barbarian. How do you know so much? Is it possible, as our Supreme Leader has told us, that your people can read minds? Are you reading my own mind right now? If this is true I must bring you to the attention of the torturers right away."

Zaor and I looked at Shamar questioningly, wondering if the man truly had this power to read minds—and even more so, if he had read our own minds? He had not admitted this before—quite the opposite in fact. I began to wonder. The thought of him being able to read minds—and control them—made both of us uncomfortable, but it positively made the Blues frantic with fear. I indicated to the Kevan that he needed to say something to placate Vaar's growing panic—before the man did something violent.

"No, my friends," Shamar now told us in a quiet whisper, "I did not read Zaor's mind, nor your own, Jon Kirk. I did not even read this Blue's mind. If he has one! It is just logical with what my people know of the warlike Vognars that world-wide conquest must be their main goal, but I have only very limited mind power."

Vaar heard this and demanded, "So your threat against us was just bold and meaningless talk, Kevan?"

Shamar nodded, "I was angry. I have no power to read minds, nor to blast your minds with my own—though I wish I had."

Vaar was vastly relieved to hear Shamar's words and gave him a nasty look, but he was obviously relieved that the Kevan had admitted he had not interfered with anyone's thoughts, nor could he use his mind powers to kill. Vaar cursed us all as troublemakers, then he roughly pushed us forward towards the large dais and throne at the far end of the massive room. The chamber was so expansive that we walked for a full five minutes before we were even near the throne.

When we reached the throne, Vaar barked, "Enough of this chatter. Behold, barbarians, The Great Okvon, Supreme Leader of the Vognars."

Now that we were deeper inside the majestic chamber of the Vognar Supreme Leader we were surprised to see that it was still completely empty. It was a massive room devoid of any people other than ourselves. It seemed very bizarre.

There was a large and ornate golden throne in front of us set upon a raised dais—but it was also empty. However only for an instant were we puzzled by this vast emptiness—for I knew it all had to be illusion.

I still saw no one. Then I though I heard a light cough, and afterwards the hint of what appeared to be stifled laugher. If it was laugher, it came from more than one person.

CHAPTER 9

ARON THE ELDEST

Far away in the secret hidden city of Keva, Aron The Eldest, and the Old Ones of the Great Council were continually in conference over the crisis that had come upon their city and their world of Ares. They were hard at work exercising their mental powers in a vast mind-meld to infiltrate the thoughts of the Vognars. They were seeking to learn all the deadly secrets of these mysterious Blues. It was long and difficult work.

"Our people are making progress. We are finding out how to discover the powers of the Vognars, how to fly their airships, build and use their mighty beam weapons, and of course, the small box they wear that creates invisibility. That is a special device, it was something left over from the ancient peoples of Ares."

"A device?" one of the Old Ones asked curiously.

"A small machine, it bends the waves of light. It appears to be magic, but it is not, it is super science from the Ancient Ones of long ago," Lanus stated.

Now all listen," Aron said, calling for everyone's attention. "Olar has something of great importance to tell us."

Slowly a younger Kevan man rose to his feet. He looked to be a serious sort, worried, and quite young for this council of aged sages. Olar was indeed youthful in age, having lived a mere 50 years of life as compared with Aron's more than 800 years of life. Nevertheless, he was a valued council member with very special talents. Now all eyes were turned to him in anticipation of the news he had to report.

Olar took a deep breath and carefully began his report to the Great Council of the Old Ones of Keva. "Through mind calculations I have been able to discover the location of King Shamar, as well as Jon Kirk and the green warrior general, called Zaor. All three are at this very moment are being held captive, and even now are in the very presence of his mighty lordship, Okvon, Supreme Leader of the Vognars. They are in the capital city of the Blues far away on the eastern continent across the Serpent Water. I and my team are making contact and shall soon have a connection with Shamar's mind in place and open for your contact with him Aron."

There was a murmur of approval and consternation among the Old Ones for this was good news, but any matter of war was disturbing for the Kevans, and this would bring them deeper into it. The eastern continent of Vognar was unknown to most green people, and it was mysterious and dangerous to the Kevans who until then had not known of its existence except in old long-lost books. Nor did they care. However, to realize that all those terrible old stories, meant to scare the uneducated and superstitious might in fact be true, was unnerving. The continent of Vognar was also so far away, many leagues across the deadly Serpent Water. How could any mind reach that far, even with many of them in a meld?

"What if this blue-skinned enemy forces Shamar to talk, or they can somehow enter his own mind? Looking for information?" asked one of the Old Ones named Laar, obviously nervous and growing fearful about Keva becoming involved in the coming war. "Then under torture he may tell them all he knows about the location of Keva and the mind powers of our people. That could doom us all. We are a small city-state, not powerful, we cannot oppose these thousands or millions of Blues."

"That is true, my friend, but true only under normal circumstances. However remember, we have powers that are not normal. We must also remember that noble King Shamar is a great warrior, not only a king of Keva. He will never give up our secrets, even under the worst torture imaginable, and we will soon have Jon Kirk and his Green Empire with us. That will make all the difference." Aron insisted firmly.

"I agree with Aron," Olar stated. "King Shamar is strong, we shall prevail."

Aron continued, "Shamar and his two companions are all valiant warriors. We will aid them, and in doing so, they will aid us. We need the Greens to fight and win this war. With this Jon Kirk, they can do it."

"I am sure Aron is correct about their bravery, no one here doubts that," Laar replied testily, "but we must remember that our numbers are too small to even contemplate any conventional fight with the blue men across the Serpent Water."

"That is why we need the Greens. I have now established a mind-to-mind link with King Shamar," Olar continued with a bold sweep of his arms. "I have told him to keep hope in his heart and that we will make our plans known to Jon Kirk and Zoar through him soon. Events are progressing well, but there is still great danger."

* * * *

Zaor and I were initially shocked when we were taken into the Vognar throne room. For there appeared to be an empty throne in an empty room. Not what we expected. Most unusual. Other than our guards, there seemed to be no one else there at all. However, I could feel a presence there. A terrible dark malignant presence.

I turned when I heard what sounded like another muffled cough, accompanied by a hint of stifled laughter. Now that we were closer I could smell perfume and the sweat of bodies. Many bodies. I realized the truth now, that vast chamber was in fact full of people—all people that we could not see.

Shamar now whispered to us, relayed words from Aron's mind speak, which gave us hope. "I am in mind-to-mind contact with the Old Ones of Keva now. Aron The Eldest tells me they are working on our problem. They will aid us, and we will be rescued soon. We are to wait, do nothing yet, and all shall be soon revealed."

I only nodded grimly. I did not like the idea of waiting for those of Keva to begin our escape, but if we were to get help, that was something worth waiting for. Help would be nice, from whatever quarter, but I was determined that help or no help, Zaor and I would find some way to escape and get back to Tarcos no matter what these Blue fiends had in store for us.

In the meantime we were led by Vaar and his guards closer to the empty throne.

Then suddenly before us the air began to shimmer and a large and grossly fat blue man suddenly appeared upon the throne. For an instant he was alone, just sitting there by himself, watching us with an amused look upon his jowly face. Then many hundreds of the enemy suddenly became visible all throughout the huge chamber. There were now row after row of them appearing. Hundreds. Perhaps thousands.

Now that they had all become visible to us, I saw there were blue-skinned people everywhere. Men and women, nobles and warriors, the entire court of the Vognar leader. Obviously they had been invisible and remained silent as we were led into the throne room, better to make the effect of their becoming visible even more impressive to us. It was. Even though we had *felt* the presence of others in that room, we had seen no one until now. Seeing them all appear like that instantaneously before our eyes now, was a shock and surprise I shall never forget.

I looked up to see the man who sat upon what had once been an apparently empty throne, a man who had suddenly materialized right before my eyes. Okvon, the Supreme Leader of the Vognars and the Blues. He was the largest man I had ever seen. He was grossly overweight, wearing rich clothing and covered in gleaming jewelry, and he oozed a malignant power. His dark blue face emanated an evil with a relentless thirst. Shamar gasped nervously. Zaor took a step back. I clenched my fists ready for whatever might come.

"Bow down to Okvon, Supreme Leader of the Vognars!" Vaar ordered us harshly, and when we did not move, his men used their weapons to force us to show the required respect.

"I bow my knee to no man," I growled, resisting the guards, adding, "and especially I do not bow down to any vile creature such as you, Okvon."

The Supreme Leader did not appreciate my words of defiance. His face grew red with furious anger but to his credit he held his patience.

Vaar glowed red with rage at this insult to his leader, and he quickly struck me with the blunt edge of his sword. "Down you filth!"

I moved quickly too now, a bit too quickly for my guards, so I dodged his blade, and then gave Vaar a hard fist into the face. I was growing tired of games and of these insolent Blues. Vaar reeled then fell down to the floor.

"Hah!" Zaor laughed at the Blue. "Not so tough now, eh?"

Vaar, the Vognar officer had fallen to the ground stunned, but after a moment he rebounded and ordered his men to punish me for my attack upon him. He told his men to hit me mercilessly, it was an effective beating even though I got in quite a few effective shots back at my tormentors. Shamar and Zaor fought to escape and help me but they were held firmly by their guards and could only watch helplessly as I received my beating. Vaar watched with evident delight, a wicked leer upon his face.

Finally the Supreme Leader, Okvon himself intervened, "Enough! Stop it! I do not want him dead, Vaar! Not yet."

"Yes, My Lord," Vaar replied and he immediately called his men off me.

The Vognar leader looked closely upon the three of us and motioned that we be brought even closer to the throne so that he could view us better. When we were closer, we were halted before the Supreme Leader by Vaar and his guardsmen and held there. I considered trying a surprise attack upon Okvon to take the Supreme Leader hostage, but held back for the moment. I wanted to find out what information I could gain from him first, and I also decided to wait for the help we were promised from the Kevans. I did not want to do anything to interfere with, or mix-up, their plan. They said they would help us and I appreciated that help. I just wondered what that help could be, seeing that it was aid coming from so far away across the vast ocean and from the other side of Ares. I wondered what they could do to help us from so far away.

Okvon looked at me closely now with open contempt. "So you are the upstart fool who dares call himself emperor of all Ares? You are the man called Jon Kirk?"

Okvon was obviously highly insulted and angry by my title, for he viewed himself as the only one to lay claim to any important title on Ares.

I looked the Blue leader in the eyes boldly, my eyes blazing back with fierce defiance, "I am he, but I did not seek the title, it was forced upon me by the people I serve. I only accepted it to better lead the green peoples against their enemies and to freedom."

"The Greens? They are nothing, it is the Blues who are important and who shall rule!" Okvon shouted, the fatty folds of his face and jowls shaking with rage with each word. "And now, Jon Kirk, what manner of being are you? You have neither blue nor green hued skin, nor are you a Zaran winged man?

"I am an American, from Earth," I replied simply with pride.

"Am-Racan? Er-Arth?" Okvon shrugged, pronouncing the words like most on Ares would do so, in two syllables. "What strange country are these? I have never heard of them, but it is of no consequence. However, when it comes to the title of emperor of Ares, there is another more fit than you for that position, Jon Kirk, and that is, of course, myself. Hah, why even the noble Grusus, the new king of the winged hordes has a more valid claim to that title than you do. The Winged-men, our new allies. Even now he and his army are carving up your middling Green Empire, even as his swords and daggers carve up the green people of the eastern continent who oppose us."

I grew enraged by these words and the knowledge that the Blues were working together with the Zaran Winged-men, but I held back my rage. For the moment.

There was general laughter throughout the chamber against the Greens by the Blues at their leader's striking remark.

Zaor, Shamar and I coldly stared at Okvon after his stunning and cruel words, though we prayed those words were false, or that the Vognar plans would never come to pass. We feared for the green people in the light of such dangerous enemies. I thought of my beloved Sirah back in Tarcos, and prayed she was safe and that the city had not yet fallen.

"By now," Okvon said with a renewed eagerness as if reading my fears, "Tarcos will have fallen. Soon that city, and your so-called Green Empire, will be but a memory. Mentep, come forward!"

In response to the Supreme Leader's command, from the front rank of Vognar nobles and warriors, strode forward a middle-aged huge blue-hued warrior. His rank denoting him as a high officer in the Vognar military. Lord Mentep was, in fact, the Lord Admiral of the Vognar air fleet, and he would lead the Vognar horde's invasion to take over the eastern continent. He was also the brother of Okvon.

"Yes, my Lord," Mentep answered bowing before his lord and Supreme Leader.

"You, my loyal brother, Lord Mentep," Okvon ordered firmly, "shall take command of our expedition tomorrow and crush all resistance on the eastern continent of Ares. Soon we shall conquer the entire planet. Your army shall also aid Grusus in every way possible in his war against these green scum."

"Yes, Supreme Leader!" Lord Mentep replied obediently.

"However, these winged creatures are strange beings, not of Ares originally, so if Grusus and his flying followers refuse to aid our horde in your conquest, or become treacherous or cowardly, you have my permission to destroy them one and all. Then take full control of the eastern continent of the green people for me here in Vognar. Remember the winged beasts are our allies in this coming war—but it is only an alliance of convenience for us. We shall turn upon them when they are no longer useful. Ares is our world, the winged creatures are interlopers here!"

"Yes, My Lord," Mentep replied eagerly. "The warriors stand ready to fight and die in your service, Great King."

"As they should, Lord Mentep. I trust you with the destruction of the Greens. In fact, once we conquer that land, I think I shall change the name of the continent of Cos to 'Okvon', in honor of myself and my heroic conquest."

"That is a superb idea, My Lord, and it shall mark your great victory for all the ages," Mentep said with fawningly effect. "I know it is a most fitting and noble name for our newly conquered lands."

Okvon smiled with pleasure at these words. Then he looked at me and added, "Perhaps, afterwards, we shall even find this country of the white-skin here, this Am-Racan, or Er-Arth, or whatever it is, and conquer it as well!"

"Yes, my Lord, more lands to conquer is a fine plan for the future. Your people will love to have the newly conquered eastern land blessed with your noble name, all in honor of their beloved Supreme Leader."

I looked to Zaor and Shamar and gave both men a twisted grin. Shamar slowly shook his head, while Zaor tried to hold back a biting comment.

Nevertheless, a loud applause soon arose from those Vognars assembled in the huge chamber. Shamar, Zaor and I did not try to hide our laughter at the bombastic egotism of the Vognar leader. He had to be delusional or mad, or both.

Okvon heard us, his face took on a twisted visage as he looked upon the three of us with rage and hatred. We were raining on his parade and I was glad of it. He was a man never to be ridiculed. He sharply bellowed, "Enough! Take these barbarians away from my majestic presence! My eyes burn at the very sight of them any longer! Take them away from me and have them killed, but make sure that it happens very slowly and very painfully."

Bold words from a big coward!" I shouted out defiantly, purposely insulting the enemy leader, hoping to egg him on.

There was a deadly hush throughout the massive chamber. The people were shocked and astounded by my incredibly defiant words.

"You dare challenge me!" Okvon growled in rage.

"What are you doing?" Zaor whispered to me nervously. I motioned him and Shamar to be silent and to go along with my plan.

I saw my opening.

"Yes, I challenge you!" I shouted boldly.

"A challenge? A challenge! I have not had a challenge in a very long time. No one has ever been foolish enough to post a challenge to me in so long a time," Okvon replied thinking it through with some amusement, an evil leer overcoming his face.

I looked directly at Okvon, "I am the Emperor of the Greens, you are a King and Supreme Leader of the Blues, what better for the two of us to do battle to see which shall claim the true title of Emperor of Ares once and for all. I hereby challenge you Okvon, in personal combat, to the death!"

The Supreme Leader stood up from of his throne, his fatty folds quivering, his dark blue face turning beet red in rage. However, he quickly regained his composure and actually smiled. He showed pointed yellow teeth in a death's head grin, "So be it! I accept your challenge, Jon Kirk. We shall fight to the death. Let the challenge begin!"

CHAPTER 10

THE CHALLENGE

"What are you doing?" Zaor whispered to me, this time more urgently.

"A challenge. He has accepted to fight me to the death in single combat," I said simply. I expected an easy victory, Zaor realized that and finally nodded, I could see he saw the writing on the wall as well. "You have a plan?"

"There is no way I can lose," I stated simply.

"There is no way you can lose, Jon Kirk," Zaor repeated showing his sarcasim, "but I do not like it, and I do not believe it."

Shamar shook his head, "I am not sure of this plan of yours, Jon Kirk, perhaps we should wait for Aron and my people to help us escape?"

I nodded, then added, "You may both be right, but when I see an opportunity to effect our escape, or to kill an enemy leader, I take it."

Vaar and his men now roughly pushed us back from the throne and away from Okvon. I watched as the leader's bodyguard then came out into the center of the audience chamber and formed up into a large four-sided square, creating a fighting area about the size of four boxing rings, which they blocked off using their armored bodies. The guards stood there shoulder to shoulder, shields, armor and swords ready.

Lord Mentep next came forward and addressed the audience, "Let the challenge begin. Our Supreme Leader's bodyguard has marked off the fight area. The challenger should not attempt to run away when we release you, or when we give you a sword. There is no escape. Should you try to escape the fight area, the guards are ordered to cut you down immediately."

"I shall not run away, I am ready and eager to fight your Lord," I stated calmly.

"So you say now, but once you engage in battle with our valiant Supreme Leader and you taste the flash of his mighty swordplay, and see his supreme bravery, you will turn coward just as all others have done before you. Then you will be an easy kill. But you must fight and not run away."

I nodded, looking at the blue hued leader, who was so grossly overweight I wondered how he would even be able to get out of his throne to fight me.

Then I spoke to this Lord Mentep, "Has your leader fought in many sword fights before?"

"Very many, and the Supreme Leader is undefeated in all of them," Lord Mentep replied proudly, and this certainly surprised me.

I allowed a confident smirk, so this grossly overweight Supreme Leader has never lost a sword fight? That did not make any sense to me, and when things do not make sense then treachery may be afoot. I smelled a rat. A big fat rat.

"Bring the challenger into the fight area," Lord Mentep ordered and Vaar and his men brought me through the line of bodyguards and placed me at one end of the fight square. They kept Zaor and Shamar bound and well guarded behind me outside the fight box so they could not aid me or interfere in any way.

Then Vaar, grinning broadly released the bonds on my hands, and then threw a sword to the floor a few feet in front of me.

Vaar laughed boldly, "Our Supreme Leader will make short work of you, Jon Kirk."

"I think not," I growled defiant.

Vaar just laughed as he left the fight area. I walked a couple of feet and picked up the sword from the floor. It was a good weapon, strong and well-balanced, an able fighting weapon. I was pleased with it. It would soon be tasting Okvon's blood. I smiled, waiting for the battle to begin.

Then with much flourish, Okvon stood up from his throne and proclaimed to all boldly, "I accept the challenge of this barbarian outworlder. I will defeat him in battle sword to sword. I shall make short work of him. No opponent can stand against my brilliant and all-powerful swordplay. I am now ready to fight. I proclaim Tharn to be my champion!"

I looked up in surprise at that last word, blurting out, "What champion?"

My question was overpowered by the noise of eager excitement and cheers from all the Blues, who were certainly overjoyed by the announcement. It seemed they knew something I did not. Then when I saw this Tharn walk forward I realized that I had been very well snookered.

Much like Okvon, this Tharn was the largest Blue I had ever seen, but where Okvon was grossly overweight, a man with fat layered upon fat—this Tharn though of the same large size, was a giant who appeared to be made of muscle layered upon muscle. He was a monster. I looked at him as he strode confidently through the line of guards bordering our fight area. He was fully dressed in battle armor, held a small shield, and carried a long sword which he held ready in his hand. He carried his weapon effortlessly but with the confidence of much use. He certainly looked like he meant business. I was properly impressed and now very concerned.

"What is this!" I shouted again in anger. "The challenge was to you, Okvon, personally, not to your lackey!"

"Tharn is my personal bodyguard. He has never been defeated. He is my chosen champion," Okvon stated boldly to the cheers of all those present. "Such is the way civilized men settle their differences, rather than uncouth barbarians!"

I was the uncouth barbarian.

The chant went up from the crowd of Blues, "Tharn! Tharn! Tharn!"

Tharn seemed to be the local favorite here and quite popular with the people. I could well see why. So I was to be served up in a fine and bloody show. Or so they thought!

I looked at this Tharn more closely. He was surely a mountain of a man. This was not working out as I had planned. It would not prove as simple a battle as I had first thought either.

Lord Mentep now came forward, "Though it is cowardly to do so, as the challenger, you are also allowed to choose a champion to fight for you. Perhaps one of the two prisoners over there?"

Zaor shouted, "I will fight!"

Shamer barked, "This is not fair, it is not honorable!"

"How about I choose you?" I asked Lord Mentep.

The Blue lord just smiled and shook his head in feigned sadness, "No, I am afraid that is not allowed."

I nodded grimly, well I could see the way this was going. "So be it! I shall do my own fighting, I shall take on this Tharn sword to sword, blade to blade, and defeat him as I have all others."

"Good. Now are both combatants ready?" Mentep asked looking to Tharn and then over to me.

We each nodded our heads that we were ready.

Lord Mentep now shouted the command, "Let the challenge commence!"

Loud cheers instantly went up from the crowd. Tharn's name was shouted in joy with chants of victory against the 'evil barbarian.'

The evil barbarian. That was me.

I slowly moved forward, studying my opponent carefully. He was huge, maybe not so fast, but no doubt a dangerous adversary. He was one and half times my size and as a result I am sure he thought I would be easy prey. Normally that might be true, but I had my Earthly muscles and physique that gave me incredible strength and stamina here upon Ares. So in that regard, we might be equals. It was our sword fighting ability that would prove the key in this battle. I never doubted my ability in that area. I grasped my sword firmly.

Tharn looked at me and leered evilly, then he spoke up loudly for the crowd, "I shall make your death slow and painful, to entertain this fine crowd. No one ever defeats the Supreme Leader in battle!"

The crowd cheered and chanted Tharn's name in loud support.

"Hah! Some battle!" I growled defiantly.

Then Tharn shouted a loud war cry and suddenly ran at me with his sword held high in a vicious devastating blow. Our sword blades met with a loud clang of metal upon metal. Our blades struck hard and loud but I pushed him back. I had taken his hardest shot and held him off. I was feeling pretty good about that.

Then all of a sudden Tharn disappeared.

"What?" I gasped surprised.

Then I knew.

Tharn had become invisible.

"What is this!" I barked loudly to Okvon and the crowd in shock and anger. "More treachery! Invisibility!"

"This is dishonorable!" I heard Zaor shout in support from behind me.

Laugher filled the room, with Okvon laughing the loudest of them all. They all seemed to find Tharn's sudden transformation into invisibility quite amusing. I did not. I was now fighting an enemy almost twice my size and now I was unable to see him. Where was he? How could I fight such an opponent? I was in a bad fix now and knew it.

The laugher grew louder as frantically I looked around me for some way to tell the whereabouts of Tharn. There was nothing. I could see nothing. I could not find him. Where was he standing?

Suddenly I felt a slight nick upon my shoulder. I saw nothing but felt a light cut, and I saw a thin trickle of blood run down my arm. I had been blooded. I was sure that it was the first of many such cuts I would receive before Tharn finished me off. He had told me death would be long and slow, and now I understood what he meant. My slow death would be entertainment for the crowd in Okvon's throne room.

The crowd cheered wildly with delight. They were certainly a blood-thirsty bunch.

I stood back, I was scared now. How could I fight someone I could not see? I tamped down my panic and tried to get a new and effective strategy with better tactics in order. I though it through quickly. I knew what I had to do.

"Hold, Tharn!" Okvon suddenly ordered as he stood up from his throne and spoke in a loud commanding voice. "Now you see the folly of your challenge, Jon Kirk. Now you see how I will defeat you in battle. You shall fight Tharn the way we Blues fight all our opponents. Unseen! Your time has come. You will not even see death coming! Now, Tharn, commence the fight!"

"Yes, Supreme Leader!" I heard the blue giant shout in reply.

I moved back, took a read on his position and made a bold charge to where I figured his voice had come from. My sword slashed back and forth, using speed with as many quick swipes as I could get in—they were taking the place of finesse now. It did not work. I did not strike anything. Then I felt another light cut on my left shoulder. A light trickle of blood ran down my left arm this time. I had been struck by Tharn again.

The crowd cheered.

I moved back, hoping I was in a part of the fight area out of his reach. I looked at the wall of bodyguards marking off our fight area. They all had their swords out now, ready, should I move too close to them they would dispatch me as they would any coward they thought trying to escape the line. I made sure to stay away from them.

I move a few steps to my right. Where was Tharn? How could I get a location on him? There had to be a way? I concentrated on anything that might give me his location. I looked for dust trails on the floor where his feet might have moved, I listened for his footfalls, his breathing. Nothing gave me a hint of his location.

Then I heard a light footfall behind me, I quickly turned and felt another nick of his blade cut my forearm this time. More of my blood flowed but these were superficial wounds so far. Tharn was playing with me for the amusement of the crowd and the crowd cheered his every move.

I had to concentrate. At the same time I became a whirlwind, slashing madly with my sword all around me in an attempt to keep Tharn away from me—or with any luck to actually connect against his body. All I sliced was a lot of empty air.

My sword hit nothing. Tharn was too fast and made sure to keep out of my range. He could see me, but I could not see him. That meant I was at a terrible disadvantage. I was getting desperate. Then he cut me once more, this time a bit more deeply. The crowd roared their approval and I realized I had better do something soon or I was doomed. I would not go down like this! I shook off all negativity. I still lived, and where there is life there is always hope! I steeled my heart for victory.

I slowly moved off, wary, keeping myself moving around the fight area, my blade clearing the air before me as I moved, concentrating now on sounds made by Tharn. My mind and ears blocked out the sound of the crowd, their chants, my footfalls, my breathing, instead concentrating entirely on Tharn. I heard his light footfalls, but these were hard to determine a location because he was moving fast too now. He did not stay still, neither did I.

Then I heard the sound of something, it was one of his accouterments. It came to me slightly, so lightly, but I knew now that it was the sound of a metal ring clanging lightly against a leather belt. I knew Tharn wore a leather harness and upon it was one metal ring used to attach items such as a dagger or small pouch. I heard the sound and concentrated upon it to the exclusion of all else.

Now I had a read on his position and I feigned hapless confusion, turned my back to him, then when I heard him come at me, I swung around and thrust my blade upwards in a bold stroke. It was a great move. Had he been visible to me, Tharn would have fallen down dead at my feet.

However, it was not to be. My blade missed. It only slashed empty air but then I saw something very interesting that made up for my missing sword strokes. It was just a tiny flash, instantaneous almost, and then gone. I wondered what it was. What had I actually seen?

I moved off, perplexed. I forget about the metal ring now. This was something else, much more interesting and perhaps even more crucial to my survival. I moved away, again, I always kept moving even as my mind raced and tried to make some sense out of what I had seen. I allowed a slim grin now, for I think I new what it was. What it was, was a chink in Tharn's armor of invisibility and I made ready to exploit it.

I moved off keeping my blade always moving in front of me in an attempt to block his own blade, turning, always turning, as I tried to stay away from Tharn, as I thought this through to set up a trap.

Tharn came at me again and cut my left forearm. I winced in pain but smiled for I had seen that flash again. I saw it clearly this time. I moved away. The crowd cheered. I kept moving. Now I knew what I had seen, it was the very small tip of Tharn's sword blade. Just the visible tip of his blade—but it was enough! It told me everything I needed to know.

I quickly moved off, always keeping moving, trying to figure this out and how I should play it. I realized now that somehow Tharn's invisibility only extended to cover his body, along with perhaps an area *surrounding* his body of a foot or so in every direction. No more. That meant his body, along with, say a foot of space around every part of him, was invisible. Which meant that anything that extended outside the area of his body, like the tip of his sword, would be visible. What I was seeing was the tip of his sword point as he came at me with his blade. That was because his arm was extended away from his body in his cutting blow. His large sword now extended outside of the invisible protection zone surounding his hand and fingers. I knew I had him now!

I moved away, kept moving. Listening for Tharn. I knew he was coming at me again now. I heard the metal ring, and this time I reacted quickly and suddenly dropped down and rolled across the floor. I heard his heavy sword slam with a loud clang into the polished floor of the audience chamber. Broken granite chips from the floor flew up into the air, but the floor was all he hit that time. I was safe. He had missed me and I quickly moved off. The crowd booed his miss, and I knew Tharn would come at me all the harder now because of it. I had showed him up!

I kept moving. I knew he was coming. I got a bead on his direction from a slight ding of the metal ring on his belt, he was coming at me from the right side. I waited, then dropped down again, rolled across the floor. His sword came down, and this time I clearly saw the metal tip of his blade. That was all I needed to get a position on him.

I instantly plunged my sword upwards to the left and it struck something, hard flesh and muscle, I hoped. I pushed my blade home, deeper. I heard Tharn gasp and cry out. The crowd gasped and shouted, some of them now even cheering for me. Such is the fickleness of crowds in any life and death fight.

I heard Tharn gasp again as my blade sunk deep into him and then I heard what sounded like a death rattle. There seemed to be no response from my adversary now. I carefully approached the body, or the place where I thought the body was. I felt around. Yes, Tharn was dead. I grasped his body and moved it, and as I moved it, it left behind a heavy red smear of wet blood upon the polished throne room floor.

"Okvon screamed in rage, "Tharn! My Tharn! The barbarian has murdered Tharn!"

Lord Mentep quickly came forward with a group of blue warriors and ordered them to disarm me and hold me captive. Then he went to Tharn's invisible body, dug around a moment for something on his waist, and then Tharn suddenly became visible again. I could see Tharn clearly now. He was dead and a bloody mess. My blade had found the center of his chest, pierced his heart.

I nodded, this was good. I now allowed a grim smile because I had just learned something very important. I realized that the secret of how the Vognars were able to become invisible was definitely because of some type of device they wore. That knowledge would prove most useful.

Lord Mentep ordered the guards to take me to Vaar and his men, "Take this barbarian away!"

"Away!" I shouted, "I won your fight! I should be set free!"

Lord Mentep looked at me harshly, "You were not supposed to win. Take him away!"

"Where is your honor!" Zaor shouted in anger.

Vaar and his guards only laughed and immediately grasped my bound arms and brought me away from the fight area. Then he made sure Zaor, Shamar and I were quickly hauled out of the Supreme Leader's audience chamber and away from his exalted presence to be taken back to a large cold dark prison cell.

"You fought well, Jon Kirk," Shamar said, voicing his admiration.

"You won a noble victory against an invisible treacherous adversary," Zaor said in anger and respect. "I have never seen such a fight before, truly a battle for the ages. These Blues have no honor."

I nodded, "It was a close run thing, let me tell you. I did not expect honor from such as these. However, I did find out something about the Blues and how they are able to become invisible. They wear a secret little box-like device that they can turn on and off to make them invisible at will. It is super science, not magic."

My companions nodded, wonder shown in their faces by this knowledge of Ares super science.

Shamar nodded and told me, "Then the Old Ones of Keva are correct. They surmised such a device, something lost over the ages and left over from the Ancient Ones of Ares."

Once back in our prison cell, Zaor shrugged and pondered our fate, "We are in a dire situation, my friends, but death has no fear for me, for I am a warrior."

Shamar nodded, then added, "I am a warrior too. Okvon ordered a very slow and painful death for us, my friend. That shall not be pleasant, I can assure you. I fear they are getting their vile equipment ready for us even as we speak."

I shook my head, "We will not be here long enough for the Vognars to follow through with Okvon's torture orders. We are getting out of here now!"

CHAPTER 11

TARCOS

Faraway in the Green Empire capital city of Tarcos, an uneasy truce existed between the Winged-men and the green men of that sad and besieged city. The peace was not working as it should have, for it had merely become a waiting game. A waiting game for death.

Grusus and his flying creatures still kept the city surrounded and under siege though of course they never admitted as such, meanwhile day by day they were tightening their grip. The enemy grew stronger and more numerous each day while Sahn Jor and his force of Greens in Tarcos were growing weaker in numbers. Food was getting scarce and the water ration had to be cut again. In the meantime, Grusus had sent most of his troops to the smaller far away cities of Zoniant, Ag, Barz, and even Sfol and was in the process of conquering them all. One by one. Soon nothing would stand in his way to lay waste to glorious Tarcos itself—soon to be the lone holdout against the hated Zaran enemy.

By now thousands of winged warriors were completing their mission of the re-conquest of the other cities and even how some were returning to surround Tarcos. More were coming every day. Soon Grusus would have a force powerful enough to overwhelm the city. He was patient, he had time on his side. He was carefully and quietly moving his lines closer to Tarcos. Sahn Jor knew that the city was doomed and feared his people would eventually serve as a feast for the winged invaders. He wondered where Jon Kirk might be. Was his emperor even alive? What of Zaor?

Lady Sirah was in turmoil, sad and full of longing for her missing husband—and her missing brother. Would she ever see Jon Kirk again? Or Zaor? Would her people, who had been through so much war and travail, ever be free of the dread winged menace?

Then Sahn Jor received a message from one of his scouts telling him about the Zaran plans. It was said that Grusus had promised his army that very soon Tarcos would fall. Sahn Jor wondered what else he should do to strengthen the city defenses, and still he wondered where was Jon Kirk?

That night Sahn Jor felt the very real fear that Tarcos might indeed be lost. He knew the city could not hold out and yet thousands of brave warriors and citizens had joined together to fight for their beloved city. They had vowed to fight to the death. The Black Dragons, the emperor's personal bodyguard, had stayed loyal to a man, a thousand of the finest swordsmen and bravest fighters in the realm—but they were not enough. They might be able to hold the city for a few hours, maybe even a day, but eventually the end must come…

Sahn Jor had tried many times to get Empress Sirah to leave the city to seek safety back in the caves of the Coastal Mountains, but she would not hear of it. She would never desert her people. For always in her heart was her love for Jon Kirk and the hope that he would return to her. She could not accept the thought that he, and her brother, Zaor, might be dead. It seemed incomprehensible to her. Nor would she desert her people in their hour of dire need and desperation. No, she would stay in the city and show her people that their Empress was with them even unto the end. The Empress was so brave, and so foolish, but everyone admired her.

Sahn Jor, along with the other ministers of state of the fledgling Green Empire of Ares worked doggedly in the defense of their city. Aid from other villages and clans slow in coming for Tarcos, was now completely cut off by the siege of the winged invaders. The city was now effectively surrounded even though the treaty still apparently held. At least in theory. A treaty that held in name only—since the enemy had not yet attacked—not yet! But all knew that day was coming. The city had been in near panic for many days and some people had gone into hiding, while others even more fearful had already left the city by secret routes.

However, those who escaped Tarcos discovered there was no true escape from their relentless enemy. It turned out that many of the people who had fled the city were soon captured by the Winged-men and quickly killed, or often kept as slaves. Slavery which was worse than a quick death in battle. After a short time, no one left the city any more and a dark pall of doom descended upon the people. Everywhere streets were deserted and shops closed. The once busy and noisy streets of Greater Tarcos were now silent and seemingly dead, waiting for dawn of the day when it was said thousands of winged warrior demons would fly upon them in furious bloody swarms to capture the city and kill everyone in it.

* * * *

Meanwhile, in faraway Keva, Aron The Eldest, leader of the Old Ones was now in direct mind communication with Shamar, and through him, with Jon Kirk and Zaor. All three could now hear Aron's words.

"Tomorrow," Aron told the three captives quickly, "Tarcos will be attacked by the winged horde of Grusus, even as elsewhere the eastern continent of Cos will be invaded by an air fleet of Lord Mentep's Vognar force of blue warriors. We have seen all this through our mind powers and have made our plans accordingly. We have no time left, we must act now. Very soon men will come to release you and your two companions from your prison, Jon Kirk. They will be blue-skinned Vognars, but they will be under our thought control. They will lead you to an airship where you can make your escape. Shamar, you must fly the ship to Tarcos as quickly as possible for the fate of the free peoples everywhere on this world depends upon Jon Kirk's leadership of his army against our enemies. Jon Kirk and General Zaor must reach Tarcos to stem the Zaran attack. Leave them off there to lead their warriors in battle. Then you must take the airship and come here to Keva, where we will inspect the Vognar ship, and find the secret behind their beam weapons and that invisibility device. Then we will use them to defeat the approaching enemy air fleet. Be quick about it! We have no time to waste."

"But I can not fly a Vognar airship?" Shamar replied softly.

Aron smiled, "Have faith in us, my king. Now you can."

CHAPTER 12

ESCAPE

Shamar had told us of his mind-to-mind communication link with Aron The Eldest and to expect release from our prison cell very soon. I asked the Kevan just how Aron intended to accomplish that from so far away in Keva and he just smiled at me and said, "Wait and see, my friend. They have powers we can not even imagine. I have never before flown a Vognar airship, but I now know precisely what to do to fly such a vessel."

"That is uncanny," Zaor said amazed.

"It surely is," the Kevan replied with a sly grin. "They have their ways. Be patient, my friends."

I nodded, we waited. Zaor and I held back on our own plans of escape for the moment.

The prison was dark and quiet when two blue-skinned men in Vognar warrior harness came to our cell, unlocked it, and released me and my two companions.

"I am Beel, and this one, is Corvo. You are free. Come with us," the first of the blue Vognars said, speaking bluntly in a rather mechanical tone as if in some dream trance. It was as if his words were spoken by another. Aron The Eldest?

Shamar told us the two Vognars were held under tight mind control by the Old Ones of Keva. The Kevans controlled every action of these Blues, their every thought, word, action and deed.

I nodded and we followed our guides.

Zaor commented to Shamar as we were led out of our cell, "That's a nice trick. When we reach Keva I will have to have Aron teach it to me."

Shamar smiled, "The secrets of Keva were not for the likes of non-Kevans."

Zaor returned a grim smile of warrior guile, for I was sure he would not let the subject drop nor allow the people of Keva to keep such powerful secrets only to themselves. Military secrets are the most fleeting of all.

Soon our two Vognar guides led us to a secluded section of the palace roof, where we were taken to some kind of vessel. The place was surprisingly devoid of guards and here I thought I saw the hand of Aron and the Kevans once again. The vessel was some kind of flying ship, though much smaller than the one we had originally been in when we had first been abducted by Vaar and his men. We quickly entered the small ship and soon through Shamar's piloting knowledge, which had been borrowed from the Vognar's memory via Aron, we were aloft and racing through the blood red sky into the atmosphere of Ares towards freedom and the next battle.

* * * *

Soon after, in the vast audience chamber of the palace of the Vognars, all stood by quietly and in terror as Supreme Leader Okvon spoke to the assembled throng of Blues.

Actually, the Supreme Leader did not speak—he yelled and screamed like a raving maniac, full of rage heaped upon his trembling officers and nobles, for he had just been told that his three most valuable prisoners had somehow escaped.

"How did they axccomplish this?" Okvon demanded in fury.

"We do not know, My Lord, but…" a junior officer began, then stuttered nervously. He had been pushed forward by more senior officers to give the bad news to the Supreme Leader. Everyone knew the Supreme Leader did not ever like to hear bad news.

"But…what?" Okvon screamed in rage once again.

The junior officer withered, shook, said softly, "My Lord… the…"

"Speak up!" Okvon demanded, his anger growing—if such a thing was possible. He decided he would have them all killed, all of them who had been involved in this fiasco. He thought about it some more—even some who had *not* been involved. He did not care, he was Supreme Leader, he could do whatever he wanted to do to anyone he liked. "Well!"

"My Lord, the prisoners stole an airship."

Okvon just screamed a long chain of vile curses, heavily chastised his officers, calling them all traitors and cowards, fools and idiots. This was the final insult as far as the Supreme Leader was concerned. The prisoners had escaped in one of his own airships! Enraged, he suddenly began to call out names apparently arbitrarily and ordered the men to be put in chains and then they were ordered butchered by his guards in his very throne room right in front of him. The nobles and warriors, men and women of his court stood by aghast, forced to stay there and watch it all. It was horrible. It was hours before his taste for blood and revenge had been fulfilled.

Those of his officers and nobles who were left alive after the bloody carnage were utterly terrified, trembling with fear, wondering if they would be the next target of the rage of their insane and murderously despotic leader.

"What news of Lord Mentep?" Okvon now demanded suddenly, his thoughts quickly having turned toward the invasion fleet.

A brave young noble spoke up nervously, "We have good news to report, Supreme Leader. Very good news. Lord Admiral Mentep, with his great fleet of airships and hordes of warriors have left our capital city and by now are flying over the province of Lanar. Soon they will cross the deadly Serpent Water and then make landing on the eastern continent."

"So all is going according to plan?" Okvon asked harshly.

"Yes, My Lord, all is going according to your glorious plan," the nervous noble said trying to be positive, hoping this good news would save him from the wrath of his violent despotic leader for the time being.

It did not.

Okvon looked at the young noble, shook his head with a motion that indicated impending doom, "Not good enough, Sofon! Guards, take him away. I will deal with this one later."

Sofon screamed, "No! My Lord! Please! I have done nothing wrong! I did nothing but serve you honorably and loyally!"

Okvon nodded and allowed a death-head smile. This was a loyal young officer but he was terrified because this action taken against him had been so unexpected and unnecessary. Totally arbitrary. Okvon liked arbitrary. Sofon really had done nothing wrong. That is what made his treatment so delicious to a fiend like Okvon.

The Supreme Leader brightened and spoke up, "Take him away. Let him stew upon his fate for a time. He might offer us all a few hours of entertainment before he dies later this evening."

* * * *

Piloted by Shamar, the stolen Vognar airship with the cloak of invisibility device, quickly streaked through the thin air of Ares, taking us across the Serpent Water until we were upon the continent of Cos racing toward the gleaming city of Tarcos. After an hour we landed secretly upon the roof of the royal palace of Tarcos just as the red sun had set. It was the night before the attack on the city by the Winged-men horde the next morning and a gloom of dread covered the city. Zaor and I were anxious to get into the fight.

Shamar quickly opened the ship's airlock and Zaor and I left the vessel. The Kevan wished us good luck in our coming battle, then he got back inside the vessel and the ship took off. Zaor and I watched knowing he flew the ship towards his city of Keva. Where ever that might be.

Now Zaor and I watched the ship fly away and we sighed with relief, delighted to breath the cool crisp air of Tarcos, happy to be in our beloved city once again.

"It feels good to be back home and alive," Zaor told me in an intense tone, for I knew though he was relieved to be home there was much on his mind about the upcoming events and the battle tomorrow.

"Yes, and now we bring the fight to the enemy," I said grimly. I had waited for this moment for many weeks and it was good to be back in action again. However there was one thing that had to be done first. "I must be reunited with Sirah."

"And I too miss my mate, Manalia. The women have been very brave," Zaor stated.

"Yes, they are always brave, it gives us strength," I said as we left the rooftop.

Then Zaor and I entered the palace, walking by surprised guards who let us pass with cheers of joy at our return, and we made our way to Sahn Jor's apartment. There we found the First Minister seated with Empress Sirah and Zaor's wife, Manilia. The reunion was an emotional and teary-eyed event.

"Jon Kirk! I knew you would come back to me," Sirah cried, running to me and hugging me to her tightly. I held her firmly in my arms. It had been too long that we had been parted. It was a sweet reunion.

I saw Manalia run into Zaor's open arms and he flung her around in a mad dance of sheer joy.

"I have come back to you, my love," I said holding my dear wife closely. She felt so good, so warm, so tender and sweet to be with again.

"Yes! Yes you have, my love!" Sirah cried.

Once our sweet reunion was over Zaor and I gave our wives and Sahn Jor a short report on what we had been through the last few weeks. We told them much about Shamar and the people of Keva; the Blues, the Vognars of the western continent; and of all their super secret weapons. Then I told them about the Vognar invasion and what I planned to do about it.

"It is a risky venture, My Emperor," Sahn Jor said thoughtfully.

"Perhaps, but it will buy us time, time that we need desperately to win this war," I stated firmly. "I will lead the mission, Zaor will come with me. Sahn Jor, you must remain here, for if I am unsuccessful in this plan then you will need to rally the troops to defend the city in a last ditch effort against tomorrow's attack."

"It is a bold plan, my husband," Sirah told me softly, nervous for my safety and fearful she might lose me, even as I had just returned to her after so long a parting.

"Yes, but a bold plan is needed," I responded with a slight grin. "It will be all right. If I am successful there will be no attack tomorrow."

Empress Sirah nodded, accepting the danger that I was willing to place myself in to save the city we both loved and the people who needed us so desperately.

"Here is my plan," I stated calmly to the group of four people around me. "Zaor and I will immediately and secretly go forth from the city with twenty of my Black Dragons. We will enter the Zaran encampment and assassinate this Grusus and all other winged monsters and Vognar allies who are with him that we can find. For they are working together now. With Grusus dead it will throw the enemy army into turmoil. They will be in total chaos.

No way will they be able to launch an attack tomorrow without a leader. That will buy us the time we need."

CHAPTER 13

THE RETURN TO KEVA

Shamar retuned to that secret hidden land controlled by his home city-state of Keva and was welcomed warmly by thousands of hearty and joyous green men and women. All were happy to see their king alive and brought back to them again—and returning to them on such a wonderful flying ship. Shamar could easily see what a popular leader he had become to his people, but he also saw how they all marveled at the stolen Vognar airship that he had arrived in. Aron The Eldest was the most happy to see that wonderful airship. It was impressive and he knew it held secrets that even now the wily Kevans were breaking down, copying, and putting to use in their own weapons.

"One might think you are more happy to see this flying ship, than you are to see your own king," Shamar told wily Aron with a wink as they inspected the enemy vessel.

"Nonsense, my lad, you are our good king," Aron told him with a wry grin, "and I am happy to have you back alive and safe with us again. But I would be lying to you if I did not admit I was even more happy to have this amazing Vognar ship."

"Hah! Overjoyed to have it, is more like it!"

Aron gave a sly smile, "Yes, overjoyed is a good word for it, for I am thrilled to unlock the secrets that it holds. This ship is important to the survival of our city and our people. You have done well, my king."

Shamar gloried in that simple praise from the great Aron.

The king of Keva was next met by the full Great Council of Old Ones, and under Aron and Olar's instructions they set about examining the workings of the Vognar airship and the workings of its secret devices in detail. The information they took from the ship proved to be a treasure trove. Soon they were making their plans for the battle to come. They must work fast now for they knew the Vognar air fleet was on the way and time was precious.

"What news of Tarcos?" Shamar asked Aron once they had some time alone. "I have returned Jon Kirk and Zaor to that city, and I saw that it stood safe when I was there last evening, but does the city yet stand?"

"Yes, it stands as yet, by what we have been able to determine from our mind-to-mind searches—so far it does stand safe from the enemy," Aron replied tensely. "However, time is precious for them as well."

Shamar nodded, and he could see that the elder had a lot of problems preying upon his mind—deep dark fears were there— none saw them all clearer than Aron. Shamar was glad that he was not one of the Old Ones, he did not want to be able to see all the darkness and evil that they saw. It was too disturbing, so unsettling.

They walked on, examining the ship and making notes, comments, things to be done. So much to be done.

Finally Aron smiled and said, "A mind-search has just told us of an impending attack upon the Winged-men camp surrounding Tarcos, and that Grusus, the leader of the winged horde seems to be the target. The plan is to assassinate him in his own headquarters. If it works, this may stall the attack on Tarcos and throw the enemy into chaos for the moment. How long that lasts we can not know."

Shamar allowed a grim smile with a hint of hope, "That is good news indeed. I see the hand of Jon Kirk in that I am sure."

Aron nodded, hopeful such an attack might work, "My thoughts exactly. I wish Jon Kirk well, but we have a more serious problem now. The battle fleet of Lord Mentep of the Vognars has already landed upon the eastern continent and he plans to join forces with the winged horde to destroy Tarcos. It is as I feared, but it is even far worse. After they destroy Tarcos his mission is to seek us here in Keva and destroy this city and all the people in it."

"Then Lord Mentep's fleet must be stopped or destroyed," Shamar demanded. Then he added, "and just as important is that these Winged-men must be routed from their attack upon Tarcos."

"That is exactly what we shall do now," Aron said with a grim smile.

"But how can we do that?" Shamar asked, dubious of how it would be accomplished.

"We have ways, my king. We need to get to work right away." Aron The Eldest told him. Then he stood up and got everyone's attention and began to outline the plan that he had formulated for the war. A plan which he hoped would save Keva.

The Old Ones of the Great Council all turned to listen to their revered leader with firm determination and not a little fear. This was grim business now. They were embarking upon dangerous ground in waging this war. They knew that. They also knew that failure meant death and extermination.

Aron continued speaking to the gathered leaders in a firm and serious tone, "Nothing but a lack of speed on our part can cause this plan to fail. It all depends upon the amount of time we have to get ready and the speed with which our action is carried out. Already, even before you set foot back in Keva, King Shamar, certain forces have been put into play by us. The Great Council is ready and we have been busy while you have been gone. We now have four small airships built and ready. It was done using the old knowledge of the Ancients, but now we need to make all haste to include the Vognar wonder weapons inside these ships so we can get them set for battle. We may even be able to augment those weapons. Improve them. Then we will be ready. Once the battle is joined, we must all await the results. It will either be victory or death, life or utter annihilation, there is no third way for us now."

CHAPTER 14

KILLING GRUSUS

My plan was set. Zaor and I, with twenty of my hand-picked Black Dragons elite bodyguards exited the city of Tarcos on our mounts through a secret tunnel and came out onto the dead plains behind the city. This was the dangerous no-man's land between Tarcos and the lines of the enemy horde of Grusus who held the city under siege.

We rode hard out upon the plains outside the city the few miles towards the horizon and soon reached the Zaran lines. As we approached the enemy camp I had our small column slow down. Zaor and I rode a bit closer to the enemy and when I found the right position, I quickly had the column come up and then stop at a tall sand berm where I ordered my men to dismount. We checked the area to be sure there were no enemy scouts around. So far the area was clear of any guards or pickets. I smiled knowingly, the Zaran's as always, were so over-confident. They saw themselves as so superior and would never believe the Greens would ever have the audacity to mount an attack upon them now. That confidence would be shaken this night if I had anything to say about it.

I left two Black Dragons to hold our mounts secure and quiet. Then with Zaor and the rest of my men we gathered together into a small huddle and I went over our plan one more time in a low whisper.

"I am here for one reason and one reason only, to kill the leader of these winged monsters, Grusus. Zaor will come with me, for I may need his help."

The Black Dragons nodded approvingly. They liked bringing war and bloodshed to our enemies. I could not disagree with them.

I looked at Zaor, he smiled grimly, as ever ready for action.

"This will be a difficult and dangerous task. You men will accompany Zaor and I into the enemy camp. Your job will be to run interference for Zaor and myself, and block Grusus's men, so that I can have the time I need to get to him—and kill him. Once Grusus is dead, you are to gather into your two-man teams, then strike out on your own for a short time creating as much murder and mayhem in the enemy camp as possible. You all have fire starters?"

The men nodded, smiling, knowing what the plan was. The small device would create an instant open flame when flicked. It was much like a cigarette lighter I had used back on Earth and would come in very handy this night. It was a present to me from Tar-gool long ago, and I had had many copies made and distributed to my men. They would prove useful on this night's brutal business.

"Good. When the time is right make your flames and set everything in the enemy camp afire. On your way out cut down as many of the enemy as you can, do as much destruction and damage to them as you are able. I not only want this Grusus dead, I want the Zaran horde completely in chaos so it will take them days to get their force back in order and for them to find new leadership. That will buy us and Tarcos the time we need to win this war."

The men nodded, they were ready and eager, swords and knives were silently drawn from oiled scabbards. This would be silent work to begin with, we would be as the shadows in the dark, unseen and obscure, and the Winged-men would never know what hit them.

"Silence is the word," I stated.

"We are ready, Jon Kirk," Zaor whispered with a sly grin. The men nodded, eager.

"Good, then move out," I ordered softly, and my men silently and quickly followed me over the sand berm and then down into the dark Zaran camp.

The enemy had seemingly posted no guards. I was surprised by this, but then again not so surprised, for it was ever the Zaran way to believe steadfastly in their vast superiority. An unrealistic overconfidence that seemed to be a part of their very nature. I would gladly take advantage of that overwhelming confidence this night.

"Follow me," I whispered and my men moved forward with me.

We entered the war camp of the Winged-men of Zar, a large area full of many-colored tents much like a Bedouin encampment I had once seen on Earth. There seemed no logic or order to the camp design or layout. I looked around and saw many opportunities, a treasure trove for destruction, but I grew concerned for I did not know where the tent of Grusus lay and that was my main mission this night.

Then Zaor grabbed my arm and drew my attention to a section of the encampment that seemed separated from the rest of the tents. It looked like a walled off area separated from the rest of the camp. That had to be our destination.

Zaor whispered, "The tent of Grusus?"

I smiled, whispered back, "Yes. Let's go!"

The camp was dark, we were silent. The winged monsters were asleep in their tents as my small group quickly made our way to the tent of Grusus.

There were four guards on station at the four corners of the wall surrounding the huge tent, and two more at the front entrance. My men took them all out quickly and silently. Sharp knives across unsuspecting throats and never a sound uttered.

Once we had the outside of the leader's tent secure, my Black Dragons posted themselves around the outside wall of the structure. There was no way anyone was getting into that tent now, other that Zoar and myself.

"Let's go, "I said to Zaor simply and we entered the enemy leader's tent together.

The two guards inside we expected, but they did not expect us. Zaor and I made fast work of them. They died quietly and we hid the bodies.

Inside the huge enclosure, it seemed like some rich man's mansion with one room after another, each privately separated by heavy cloths of brocade type material that in effect created walls for each of the rooms. I motioned to Zaor, we had to be quiet, for sound traveled easily in such a place. We quietly began our search.

Where was Grusus? I began to get a bad feeling. Dark doubts came into my thoughts. Was he even here at all? Had our intelligence been wrong? Had our scouts made a mistake seeing him here when he was not here? Or had he been called away?

I looked at Zaor with concern.

"I am sure he is here," Zaor whispered.

I shook my head, I was not so sure.

Zaor and I quickly but carefully walked through the various chambers of the huge tent. Most of the rooms or separate sections were empty, it was frustrating. In one room we did see a warrior sleeping and I thought this might be Grusus, but it turned out to not be the Zaran leader. Zaor cut his throat quickly and most efficiently and we moved on.

We went into another room of the tent, and here we found ourselves in a room of green females, slaves who were chained and sleeping. This posed a problem, but they must be freed. I motioned to Zaor and he understood and nodded acknowledgement. He quickly went to release the women as I went into the next and last room of the huge enclosure. I knew Zaor would carefully wake the women and quietly, one by one, free them.

While Zaor did his work, I entered the last room alone. It was the largest room in the tent, and it was lavishly furnished. It was a room fit for a king and it even had a throne at the far end—and upon that throne sat the largest Winged-man I had ever seen. He was slumped down upon the throne asleep or unconscious from strong drink. I hoped it was the latter because he was a large hulking brute and if he was drunk it would be much more easier and quicker for me to dispatch him. For I did not have a lot of time for fancy fighting this night.

Suddenly the huge winged creature batted his mighty wings extending them broadly, the terrible flapping sound sending a twinge of terror through me. I approached the creature with my sword drawn and ready. I approached carefully and looked upon the monster most intensely to make sure he was not awake. I sighed, it was hard to tell. I looked at him closely, it was most certainly Grusus. He was silent and motionless and I thanked my lucky star that he appeared to be at my mercy.

Then his eyes suddenly opened wide and his fire red pupils stared at me with sheer hatred. He smiled an evil grin full of pointed yellow teeth, "You must be the one called Jon Kirk?"

"I am Jon Kirk, and you are Grusus?" I said maneuvering myself closer, careful now that the element of surprise was lost to me.

"I am Lord Grusus, the king here," he snarled.

I raised my sword and ran towards him with murder in my heart.

Grusus was now up and ready for my attack with drawn sword. He did not call for any guards which I found surprising. He was a large hulking brute and as all Zaran's I assumed he believed he would make short work of me with his sword. He wanted me in battle solely for himself to kill. It would be a glorious kill in his eyes. So be it! He was welcome to try!

"Come on, your time has come!" I growled sharply.

"Your death is near puny man," the Zaran grunted, then he charged me full on with sword wildly chopping at my body—or the empty air where my body had been but a second before. He was quick but I eluded his best thrusts, parried his vicious cuts and slices, then returned his attack with one of my own.

Now my blade wove a tapestry of blood in and out of his guard, cutting him in multiple spots, but I could never seem to get in the killing blow. In fact, my cuts only seemed to enrage the huge winged monster all the more. He came at me harder and faster, but still he did not call for any help or guards. So, it appeared that our battle this night would be personal and private, just the way we each wanted it. That was good. However, even should he call for his guards to help him now, my Black Dragons were posted outside and positioned to stop that help from coming. Grusus would be surprised that he would get no help this night now. Not before I cut him down and achieved my mission.

"You will die and I shall mount your head on a pike in front of my tent," Grusus bellowed in rage. I was sure we could be heard now and that the sounds of our battle would alert the camp soon, so I had to act quickly.

"I don't think so. Maybe it will be I who mounts your head upon the main gate of Tarcos," I growled back. I could see he was growing fearful, even doubting his advantage and superiority over me. He was after all, so very large, but I had Earthly muscles and that was my secret weapon here on Ares. It made me far stronger than any man my size, and those Earthly muscles gave me incredible strength and stamina. Grusus was tiring but I was just getting stared. He could not understand that he had not been able to kill me yet. However, time was of the essence. I knew I had to get this bit of work done soon.

Then I saw my opening. He came at me with a wild overhead blow, missed me as I sidestepped his blade almost effortlessly.

"Stay still!" he growled in frustration.

I answered with my sword, weaving it through his guard, seeing my opening and sinking my blade down into his chest. I plunged the blade down deeper into his heart. Grusus looked at me in total abject surprise. He could not believe I had bested him in fair and honest mortal combat. I used my boot to push his body off my blade and Grusus sank down to the floor of his tent.

"And have no worry, Grusus, I shall not take your head to mount upon the main gate of Tarcos, for I do not want such a ghastly trophy from any vile creature of Zar to desecrate my city with its foul presence." This I told the Zaran leader in a bitter tone as I watched him die upon the floor in a growing pool of blood.

Just then Zaor ran into the room, his concern turned to a grim smile as he took in the scene before him, "Well, I see you did not need my help, Jon Kirk. He is dead?"

"He is dead," I answered, cleaning the blood off my blade using the clothing of the creature I had just sent to the Afterworld.

"Good, then let us get out of here. The women are free, four of your Black Dragons are bringing them back to where we have left our mounts. The rest of our men are causing massive mayhem all over the enemy camp, setting fires, cutting down Zarans. It is total chaos. Lovely, truly it is."

And it was only then that the sudden sounds of fighting and horror which had been going on all around me now made sense and I heard and understood the cries of fear and terror, the sounds of battle, and saw the flickering of flames for the first time and understood what it all meant. Now the smell of smoke and burning material, and of burning bodies came to me, and it was growing thick and heavy.

"Jon Kirk, your men found more prisoners locked in cages in the center of the enemy camp and they were also released and are now free. These prisoners are being sent back also," Zaor told me as we ran out of Grusus's tent and into the streets of the Zaran camp. "We may have to ride back to Tarcos double or triple on a mount, but we can take back all the slaves and prisoners we have freed. We have done good work this night."

I nodded, "Come on, we have a little time left before we must join the others, let us do a little more mayhem and destruction before we head back to our mounts."

Zaor smiled, "Yes, let us!"

Then Zaor and I rampaged throughout the Zaran camp causing murderous mayhem among the enemy. We cut a bloody swath through the winged defenders. Even when in the air, they had to come low to fight us, and we were there waiting for them with bloodied blades. It was carnage but it had its function. By now, the camp was in absolute chaos. My plan had worked better than I could have expected and I was happy. Grusus was dead, the slaves and prisoners were set free, and the enemy was is total disarray. They would never be able to mount any attack on Tarcos tomorrow, and perhaps not for many more days.

"Let's get back, Zaor, we have done enough here tonight."

"Yes, Jon Kirk," Zaor replied with a grim look, "it has proved to be a most enjoyable evening after all. I Thank you."

CHAPTER 15

CHAOS

It was three days later and Grusus was a bad memory now and Bron had fought his way up the ranks to become the new Zaran leader. It had been three long days of battle for power among the winged leadership before Bron and his forces had captured victory and consolidated leadership of the mighty horde.

Bron was a huge red-eyed winged creature who sat upon the gem-studded throne formerly occupied by Grusus, eyeing a prisoner being brought before him. He sat like a great gargoyle, ugly and dark, leather wings flapping with joy and delight at the helplessness of the green prisoner. Wine drooled down his thick beard as the terrified unfortunate was dragged forward to him in chains. Many of these green people were citizens of newly captured cities brought to the camp in the last couple of days. Others were from Tarcos itself, who in escaping the city thought they would be free of the Winged-men. They were not. It was said they had jumped from the boiling pot into the boiling kettle. This lone man was none of those however, he was a scout named Tam.

Along with Bron sat a dozen other winged creatures, these were the officers in his army and the nobles of his court, but there was also one mysterious man with blue hued skin whose gold collar denoted him as a nobleman and Vognar agent. He was the only such Blue to have escaped the attack on the camp by Jon Kirk and his Black Dragons three nights before. While Bron ruled now, he had not yet set the time of attack on Tarcos. So Jon Kirk's actions had held off the attack for the time that was needed.

"Drag that green animal closer, Trul," Bron shouted to his officer. "Let me get a good look at the savage."

Quickly and with extreme roughness the prisoner was released from his chains and under heavy guard brought before Bron.

"Why do you stupid cattle refuse to surrender to us? You think you can stop us by murdering our leaders? That will not stop us, we will always have a new leader. We have held you green scum in thrall for a thousand years, since we first came to your stinking world, but now you have become belligerent and defiant. Tell me why?" Bron growled in rage.

"Jon Kirk shall beat you all in the end, then Ares shall be free of you winged monsters!" the green man shouted defiantly.

Bron shouted back, "Monsters! It is you who are the monsters, the vermin! And this bandit, Jon Kirk, he shall get what is due him shortly. He can not hold out against us, we have superior numbers, fresh troops under my command who have just come into the war from our home world of Zar. Very soon now our blue-skinned allies from the land across the Serpent Water—the Blues from the eastern continent called Vognar—shall arrive in great airships with a massive army to level your city and its stupid people with it. It will not be long now, and the Greens will be gone forever."

Tam, the green Tarcos scout just stood his ground bravely, a contemptuous look upon his face for the bloody winged murderer before him. This is not what the winged leader expected. He wanted to see fear and terror. Not bravery and defiance. Patience and mercy were other qualities the Zarans neither possessed, nor understood.

"Speak!" Bron demanded in rage. He was one used to showing insolence but not one used to receiving it. Especially not from a mere green man.

The warrior prisoner remained silent, but his eyes burned with an intense hatred and fire for revenge. Tam was a scout and a proud warrior, and such a man never gave up any information to the enemy. He was ready to die. He knew what was to come. He welcomed death knowing that his mission had not been compromised.

"Answer the leader, slave!" a winged officer barked at the green prisoner as he struck the man across the face drawing blood.

At that point Tam boldly spit full into the face of the astonished Bron, then he laughed boldly. Now all there could see and hear his insult to their leader. It was something that must be answered and dealt with immediately.

The winged officer holding Tam turned pale at this dire affront to his much feared leader and master. However, it was Bron himself who flew into an insane and bloody rage. Instantly the winged leader drew his dagger and grasping the green man by the hair pulled his head back and promptly slit his throat. Then Bron sat back down upon his throne and looked upon the rest of his warriors with deadly malice.

"Remove this trash from my site!" Bron barked to his guards. Once Tam's body had been taken away, Bron looked upon the winged officer who had allowed this terrible insult by the prisoner to his royal person. Bron was still burning with rage. He quickly drew his sword and lopped off that officer's head and wings. It was three quick, clean blows and the officer's head rolled away on the tent floor, the eyes looking with sad surprise at what had just happened.

"Remove this fool's body from my presence!" Bron ordered another nervous Zaran officer. "Then put his head on a pike at the entrance to my tent to discourage other fools in my service from allowing their master such insult from any Green ever again."

Slowly the procession of winged warriors filed out of Bron's presence until the tent was empty, but for one other. All was quiet now as Bron sat in confidence with the blue skinned Vognar ambassador. They spoke in whispers about the coming attack on the city the next morning. Perhaps. The Blue was anxious and pressing Bron to attack right away, even today, but Bron wanted to bide his time. He was in no rush and wanted to consolidate his power as the new ruler. He also wanted the Blue air fleet to arrive so they could do most of the work for him to level the city.

* * * *

I knew our killing Grusus and his various lackeys would spread terror through the besieging horde surrounding the city of Tarcos. It gave hope to the green people and terror to the winged horde of invaders. The pressure upon Tarcos now was temporarily relieved to the point where Zaor and I could begin an even bolder attack on the invader's camp. This would be the battle we had waited for. All I needed was to hear from Shamar and Aron with news that their flying ships had met and destroyed the Vognar airship fleet. That was the plan, but Zaor and I did not feel too confident of it. Nevertheless, the green people of Tarcos and every one of my Black Dragons were ready and out for blood and revenge. When the time came we would attack the unsuspecting enemy surrounding our city with a rage and anger that would put the enemy host into utter chaos.

I knew that even though the enemy had a new leader in the creature called Bron, it now appeared to me that my greatest fear had come true, the winged demons had been newly reinforced from their home world of Zar. This was terrible news. It was one reason why the enemy seemed so bold and over confident now. They not only had reinforcements, they had powerful allies from their home world, and even more allies in the Blues from Vognar. The way they saw the situation they could not lose this war, and they might be correct.

Perhaps I could make that confidence work to our advantage one more time? I knew the enemy now would never expect another attack from the Greens. I also new that sometimes the best strategy was to do exactly what your opponent never suspects. So I gave the order and our forces hit them hard in the early dawn, just as the red sun of Ares rose in the sky. It was apropos, for the blazing red sun would augment the blood drenched plains where the battle was to take place.

Our horde, lead by Zaor and myself, with a thousand Black Dragons cavalry in the vanguard hit the Zaran lines just before the Ares sun rose. It was begun in the eerie half-light before morning, when vision is suspect and shadows abound. It is a superstitious and unnerving time to be attacked. We hit them hard in the center of their line behind the city—but left the rest of their line intact—while my cavalry concentrated on running down the Zarans across their own line. Those that fought died. Those that took to flight were immediately taken down with arrows by our archers. The rest of their warriors around the city remained in position waiting for orders, while we massacred their brothers behind the city. Then we rode across the line to the front of the city as the enemy fled. Behind us were thousands of our auxiliary troops from Tarcos. They were angry and full of revenge and took it out on the enemy with devastating effect. The archers continued to inflict massive damage on any Winged-man who took to flight.

The Zaran line was quickly overwhelmed by the suddenness of our attack. They were torn apart by the ferocious cavalry charge led by Zaor and myself. They were surprised, and found themselves squeezed by our powerful mounted force. We cut them down wholesale. Our fine archers shot thousands of deadly arrows at any Zaran who tried to fly away by taking to wing to gain flight, or to fight us above from the air. This day their ability to fly did not help them in battle against our deadly arrows. Our arrows forced them to stay and fight on the ground, which is just where I wanted them to be.

Now our foot soldiers moved in to cut the enemy down, even as my mounted cavalry decimated their ranks. Eventually I could see that the military cohesion and purpose of the Zaran host seemed to melt away. Panic set in. They were the masters of Zar, they were not to be beaten in battle by mere Greens—but we were tearing them to pieces now.

Now I rode at the head of a small band of Black Dragons giving chase to a group of Zaran Winged-men trying to make a break for freedom. They were smart enough not to take to wing, where our archers would shoot them out of the sky, so they ran away to the west. I knew that the creature at their head had to be their new leader, Bron. I called him out.

"Bron, you coward! Come and face me in battle!" I barked as I spurred my mount closer to catch up to him and his group. My small contingent of Black Dragons bodyguard following quickly in my wake.

I reached Bron and he suddenly stopped and turned to face me in battle. We squared off against each other. Around us his warriors fought against my Black Dragons in a brutal and bloody melee. Bron and I moved in closer, swords ready, thirsty for blood.

Bron came at me with a powerful attack but I knocked aside his sword with my blade. He was shocked I had thwarted his bold advance. I then came at him and he moved off, but I stopped him and my sword blade cut his leg, so he could no longer get away from me.

"Now you have to stay and fight!" I barked full of the fury and rage of battle.

"I will feast upon your heart, Jon Kirk!"

The creature from Zar screamed bloody murder and then came at me again with his sword swinging, just missing me. I sidestepped his mighty blow and gave him another cut, this time on his sword arm. He was done and he knew it. It was only a matter of time.

Then he surprised me, he flapped his massive wings and suddenly took to the air. That was unusual and unexpected now because our archers had pretty much kept the enemy from taking to flight—and when they did fly they were quickly shot down dead. But I was surprised when I did not see any of our arrows hit Bron.

Where were the archers?

Bron now flew above me unheeded, he flew overhead around and high up, then he dived down upon me with his sword extended from his arm like some mighty spear he would use to impale me. I stood awaiting his attack. There seemed to be none of our archers here now to help me. It did not matter. I waited for Bron's attack with the stoic patience of the fighting man. I knew he could take me with this move, but I had my own plan to bring him down. While he was still in the air high above me I waited for the proper moment and then I suddenly threw my sword up at him. I flung the heavy weapon upwards with all the power my great Earthly muscles could give it. The power of my arm shocked Bron, but it shocked him still further when my blade impaled itself deeply into his chest and he suddenly over-ended in flight and then crumpled up to crash down to the ground at my feet. I walked over to the last leader of the Zaran Winged-men.

"It is not over, Jon Kirk," Brom gasped with his last words of life. "We are not of Ares—we are of Zar—and we shall come back to claim from you what is ours."

"Then more Winged-men shall die," I said simply, determination in my voice and etched into my face.

"Then so be it," Bron gasped these last words as he died.

"Then so be it!" I repeated in a grim whisper, but the determination in his own words troubled me greatly. This battle was won but the war was not yet over.

I withdrew my sword from his body and wiped his blood off my blade using his regal clothing. The last leader of the Winged-men on Ares was dead and their army was done for now. Defeated totally. It was only left for my men to clean up the battlefield of stragglers and take prisoners.

The Winged-man horde was now leaderless and fleeing in a desperate route, the last remaining enemy were heading north-bound in terror to get away from my hosts and away from Tarcos. Tarcos was safe now and that was the main matter on my mind. My beloved Empress Sirah was in the city and she was safe. She had been under guard by Sahn Jor and his men in the palace. I sighed in relief that she remained safe, her safety was what mattered to me most in the world.

Zaor and I leading my elite Black Dragons mounted bodyguard then cut off the remains of the fleeing enemy force in a bold stroke that blocked their escape route northward. They were trapped and they knew it. Meanwhile thousands of arrows took down all the Winged-men who took to the air. They were doomed and realized it as well. Panic set in among the remainder of the horde. Nevertheless, our warriors were determined to keep the fleeing winged invaders running for their lives. Thousands of the enemy host found themselves trapped and were cut down by our troops with swords, or by our deadly archers. Those of the enemy that turned and still fought us were few and outnumbered, and these were dispatched quickly and without pity. Those that remained ran away in frantic flight. Any of the enemy who tried to use their wings to fly away and escape—were quickly taken down by our arrows.

"We have won a great victory today," I stated with joy and relief to my friend, Zaor.

"This is a great day for the Greens all over Ares," Zaor told me, his face flushed with the sweet taste of victory. "It is all because of you, My Emperor. It was a lucky day for Ares when first you came to our world."

I smiled, thinking of my beloved Sirah, "It was a luckier day for me, my friend."

The assembled Green warriors cheered both of us with chants of victory. For now the battle was done and won. The city and people of Tarcos were saved.

* * * *

Aron The Elder rose from his seat to stand in a majestic stance exuding firm timeless power. He spoke with conviction, "Everything has been completed now. Shamar will leave immediately for the city of Lanar where he will help Konor lead the revolt there against the Vognars. In the meantime, we shall aid them from here with our mental powers, blurring the enemy reactions, making them unable to fight or respond to his attacks. More importantly,

Lord Mentep's massive fleet of airships and army must be stopped, and now they will be."

Shamar immediately left Keva using another stolen Vognar air vessel on his mission toward the city of Lanar on the western continent where he was to find Konor and help lead the revolt of that province against the hated Vognars. Lanar had once been a free nation, now it would be so once more, the people of the city were already set to revolt because of Aron and his companions' work upon the minds of the leaders there. It was not a difficult thing for the Kevan Old Ones to accomplish this since the people of the city were already predisposed to revolt against their hated Vognar masters.

CHAPTER 16

THE AIR FLEET

The mighty Grand Fleet of Lord Mentep's Vognar airships raced southward across the Ares eastern continent of Cos toward the city of Sar. By now the Blues had heard of their winged allies major setback at Tarcos, the murder of Grusus days earlier, and this very day the death of Bron and the defeat of his forces. They had had a bad time of it. They were astounded of course, but that did not matter to them now. The mighty Vognar airships fl ew quickly and low above the ground over the eastern continent, a fleet of so many ships containing a massive army of blue warriors bent on conquest and gaining booty. They were anxious for easy and fast victory. They felt that victory was within their grasp and that nothing could stop them now.

Lord Mentep's smaller scout ships brought back detailed news of the routing of the winged warriors and the attack against them by Jon Kirk's army and his mounted warriors. They told tales of the devastation of the Winged-men by the Green's archers. The archers were a unpleasant surprise. They had proved a disaster for the winged Zarans. It seemed there was serious resistance by the Greens this time. Most unusual, but it did not matter, nothing could save them now.

Mentep scowled, firmly hitting his balled up right fist hard into the palm of his left hand in violent anger. "This is all no doubt the work of that Jon Kirk. Blast him! I should have killed him straight-away back in my brother's palace when he was our prisoner after the fight with Tharn. How on Ares did he win that fight? Now things are moving out of our control, but we will still prevail, and Jon Kirk shall pay dearly for his to our forces! I do not want him killed—I want him captured alive. Then I shall make him wish that he was dead!"

Lord Mentep was also angered because now he was forced by circumstances to change his battle plans and he knew he would have to turn his fleet around to seek out Jon Kirk's army and destroy it. He had to complete the job of his winged allies and that rankled him. Before that however, he must first send his airship fleet to attack and destroy the city of Sar. His mighty ships should take care of that puny city soon enough, and he comforted himself with the fact that this attack would not take him that much out of his way—and give him a victory to laud to his brother.

So Lord Mentep gave his captains orders to bomb Sar from above, bomb it into submission, then send in one ship to land with shock troops and kill all who might be left alive. That would take care of them nicely. It would also be his first conquest on this continent and would prove an easy victory. The first of many. It would be important though, because he could tout it as a great victory for his invasion fleet and the news would be received with cheers of joy when sent back to his brother, Okvon, the Vognar's Supreme Leader. Mentep knew Okvon well, and realized how important it was to send his brother good news of victories, no matter how small or insignificant they might actually be.

The siege of the city of Sar was short, it lasted only one hour. The Vognar airships rained down bombs upon the defenders mercilessly. The entire city had been sacked only weeks before by Grusus and his army of winged monsters. Now the Greens who had survived that attack had returned to rebuild their city and repaired the walls—even as their troops hunted down the broken remnants of bands of winged creatures that remained in the area. Many of the people of the city had fled to the surrounding hills before the attack so most of the people were still alive and safe. However, one small garrison of green warriors was cut off by the Vognar warships, these were quickly surrounded, but the valiant Greens would just not be killed off, nor would they give up. They were offering a hardy resistance and were becoming a problem.

Lord Mentep ordered one airship to land upon the ground near Sar. The ship landed and immediately unleashed a regiment of Blue warriors that quickly put the small force of defiant Greens under a heavy attack. He watched the brutal fight from above with glee, knowing that sending more good news back to Vognar would be to his benefit. This battle should be over soon too now. The swords of the Blues had now tasted the blood of the Greens for the first time since the dawn of Ares history, and they were eager for more.

However the battle around Sar was not yet done. More Greens suddenly came down from the hills and entered the fray to aid their brothers. Worse yet, reinforcements who seemed to be an advance guard from Jon Kirk's army were now moving north from Tarcos. These Greens charged down upon the surprised Blues with a enraged vengeance and wild abandon, cutting like a knife into his troops. The Blues had never fought such a furious enemy before. They were used to putting the sword to defenseless people, farmers or tradesmen, not having the sword put to *them* by trained hardened warriors full of fierce revenge for the murder of their brothers.

The battle between the Greens and Blues around Sar raged on, but the outcome that had at first seemed an easy victory for the Blues was now in serious doubt. The Blues now found themselves outnumbered and they were totally outfought. While Lord Mentep could send more troops into the meat grinder, he decided to cut his losses in order to concentrate upon the main object of his plan; crushing the vast army of Greens under Jon Kirk. He had no time for this puny fight, which he now considered to be a mere skirmish. He must destroy the army of Jon Kirk, the main part of which was still many leagues to the south. He knew he needed to clean this mess here up quickly and then be on his way.

Lord Mentep would send no more men down to the surface to fight and die. His plan was to order all his airships to fire down into the green warriors and destroy them in a massive array of bombs. This was the logical tactic to take now—or at least it *seemed* to be—but for some reason something in the Lord Admiral's mind made him decide against taking that action. The Vognar lord could not understand it of course, it was most strange, but for some reason he did not want to order any bombing—he would *not* order any bombing. It was as if some power within his deepest thoughts choked his thinking or clouded his reason. It caused him to neglect to give that crucial order. He could not understand why he did not give the order to fire, and soon he did not even care to think about the reason behind it. For some reason it did not matter to him now. It was most perplexing, but he soon forgot all about it. Afterwards the thought was entirely gone from his mind, with the result that none of his airships ever received any order from him to fire down upon the Greens and Jon Kirk's army.

That same mysterious mental power, which was now being sent mind-to-mind from Aron and the other Old Ones of Keva, soon caused Lord Mentep's airship commanders also to neglect to ask permission of their Lord Admiral to use their ship's armaments to fire down upon the Greens at Sar as well. Their thoughts were now also controlled by Aron The Eldest, and that control was created without the Vognars ever suspecting they were under the control of Kevan mind-to-mind thought powers. So no bombs were ever dropped upon any of the Greens on the ground around Sar.

Meanwhile on the ground, many of the Blues near Sar, realized that their fight was hopeless, and that they would get no further help from their airships above. They could not understand why this was, they tried to contact their commander without any reply, so they knew they were in terrible danger from the Greens. They retreated and ran back to seek refuge inside the one airship that had landed near Sar. They shouted frantically to the captain of the vessel, but for some reason the ship would not take off. The Vognar ship did not take off because the pilot had suddenly inexplicably forgotten how to fly the vessel. Something in his mind had clouded his thoughts regarding the use of the complex controls of how to pilot the airship. None of the other officers there seemed to know how to fly the vessel either. So the ship just sat there doing nothing.

Many more of the Blues, before they had ever reached their landed ship to hide, were brought down by the swift arrows of more green men sent as reinforcements from Tarcos by Sahn Jor. What was left of the Blue force now was a mere handful of the original thousand troops that tried in vain to flee out of range of the Greens and escape. They could not get away. This action had ended in disaster for the Vognar host and those that remained would soon became captured prisoners. The ship would be taken over by the Greens. All that was needed now was one more concerted bold attack.

Meanwhile Lord Mentep's vast fleet left Sar and flew onward seeking to find and destroy the main part of Jon Kirk's army before they would begin their bombing of Tarcos. However, the commanders seemed quite confused on exactly how to accomplish that mission now. There was much conflict and argument. While they argued among themselves, and until a decision was finally made, the fleet did nothing.

Aron The Eldest smiled, it was quite easy to influence the thinking of these Blues.

* * * *

Far away in the hidden city of Keva an Old One called Aron The Eldest and his companions entered a small black airship that took off and raced to Sar. They held a precious cargo, Emperor Jon Kirk and General Zaor. The ship suddenly became invisible, then it reached the city almost immediately.

Out of nowhere, the mysterious black fighting ship suddenly became visible again and set down outside the city of Sar. The ship was an immediate cause of great concern and fear as it landed, for everyone who saw it had never seen such a thing before. From everywhere eager warriors of the Green army rushed out to create defensive positions around the strange vessel. They were ready for whoever, or whatever would come out of that mysterious black airship. The locals lurked in the shadows, curious, yet fearful, too scared even to run. For in truth, there was nowhere to run from these airships if they shot down upon the people and the warriors. Many Greens wondered why the Vognar ships had not used their mighty beam weapons or bombs as they had done on their initial attack to shoot down upon the city and the Green troops. But the Blue airships did not fire. Why this had occurred no one could understand, but they were greatly relieved, for it changed the entire course of the battle around Sar.

* * * *

"No, My Lord, do not go towards it," a green warrior warned his officer, Major Tal, who had now joined the advance troops at the Sar battle site. "It is almost certainly a Vognar flying ship full of Blues. It is a trick of some kind, to lure us all out in the open where they can cut us down."

Major Tal nodded, though he did not agree with the soldier. He took a deep breath and bravely advanced toward the vessel. He was careful but he had no idea what to expect. No green man from this continent had ever seen such a strange black flying machine like this before.

Suddenly a doorway in the ship's hull opened and Major Tal swallowed hard with growing terror, not knowing what to expect. He uttered a deep sigh of relief when he suddenly recognized the faces of his Emperor, Jon Kirk, and his general, Lord Zaor.

The two leaders came out of the strange black airship and Tal ran forward to embrace his Lords and friends. Lords and friends that had seemingly returned from the Afterworld of the dead. Immediately a wild cheer when up from Major Tal and all the green warriors under his command as they crowded around the emperor and general to greet them. The survivors of Sar cheered the return of their greatest leaders. That cheer rang loudly through every throat, from the mouth of every green warrior as the green men ran forward in one mad frenzy of joy and victory. Tal let out another lusty yell of delight and came forward to meet his returned friends.

"Surely you have returned from the Afterworld!' Tal shouted triumphantly with sheer joy overtaking him. "It is good to see you both again."

"And I you, Major Tal," I said to the man, grasping his shoulder in staunch friendship. "You seem to have done well here against the Winged-men."

"Yes, your plan to kill Grusus worked. It bought us the time we needed. Now I hear that their new leader, another brute named Bron, is also dead and has been sent down into the Afterworld."

"Yes, I sent him to the Afterworld myself not long ago," I said proudly.

"Well, My Lord, that broke the back of their siege upon Tarcos, but now these blue men are here. Who or what they are I do not know but they are deadly and seem intent upon conquest," Major Tal stated.

"I will tell you about them soon enough, but for now let us get things arranged here, and quickly. We have a battle to begin and a war to win," I stated firmly.

"Yes, My Emperor, we are at your command!" Tal spoke up, his voice echoed by each green warrior there.

"Then let us ready ourselves. We attack now!" I shouted to resounding cheers.

Then with Major Tal and his men, and adding Zaor and his men, I ordered our attack on the remaining Blues and we defeated them resoundingly. The battle was quick. The Blues had lost all heart for war now and gave up resistance—they were not gong to lay down their lives for a tyrant such as Okvon when they were offered life by me if they surrendered. While many were killed, the few remaining Blues surrendered and were taken to add to our growing groups of prisoners. These were placed back into their own captured airship with the rest of Major Tal's advanced guard of troops.

"An airship? A ship that flies through the air like a winged man? That is amazing, My Emperor!" Major Tal stated when he was taken inside the captured Vognar airship to be flown back to Tarcos. Zaor and I would travel inside the Kevan black airship on our way to join up with three other Kevan airships, which we called the Black Fleet.

"It is one of many new wonders that we have been given by the Kevans, or taken from the Vognars," I had told my young officer before we took off.

"These airships are deadly to ground troops," Major Tal stated with alarm and some awe. "They are armed with heat beams and they can also shot down bombs and projectiles upon our warriors—they could have wiped us out easily but then inexplicably, they stopped firing upon us."

I nodded and smiled, "The Kevans are responsible for that I would bet. Aron and the Old Ones are using their mind-to-mind powers to interfere with the thinking of the Vognar officers so they would not order their ships to shoot upon our men."

Major Tal smiled, "That surely is a wonder, My Emperor."

I smiled, "It surely is. Now let's go!"

* * * *

The Grand Fleet from Vognar flew further south from Sar, and as it did so it was met by four even stranger mysterious black airships which closed in on them rapidly. Grand Admiral Lord Mentep was startled by the appearance of these unknown airships for he expected no such opposition to his Grand Fleet from the Greens. He was sure the enemy had no such flying vessels, and he was also sure these were not Vognar vessels that had been captured. They were something else, something new. But there were only four of them, after all. It meant nothing in the greater scheme of things and could never be a threat to his massive Grand Fleet, nor interfere with the Vognar plans.

Lord Mentep looked upon the four lonely ships coming towards his vast fleet and smiled. They were small but quick. Why, the fools were coming right at him! So much the better! It made it all very convenient. He would not have to waste time hunting them down. Though he did not know who they were, nor where they were from, he was supremely confident that his powerful armed force could handle them easily. His airships were a dozen times the size of these tiny vessels and far more numerous than this puny force of only four ships. He smiled triumphantly. While it appeared that these ships were armed, their armaments could be nothing compared to the weapons on his own mighty vessels. It was almost laughable that such a small force would even dare oppose his own great fleet. It was a grand but useless gesture. At least it would give his men something to shoot at, some action for his men before victory was declared would be acceptable. It was, after all, good for morale for his men to make some easy kills.

Lord Mentep immediately gave the order and soon his entire fleet of almost one hundred flying airships advanced at full speed towards the foolish newcomers. He ordered the Vognar fleet to train all their weapons upon the four small ships and be ready to fire upon his word. He could see that the fight was up in each one of his blue warriors and all were hungry for battle and blood. That too was good for morale.

As the two groups of airships converged they soon came to close quarters but the Vogars still held their fire. Lord Mentep wanted to see if he could entice the newcomers to surrender for he wanted to know who these new players were, and where they were from—rather than destroy them outright—if need be. However, if they did not yield soon, they would be blown out of existence by the many guns upon his mighty airships. The four mysterious black vessels continued to boldly come closer, as if they knew no fear, nor would they respond to any hail or orders from Lord Mentep's flagship.

"They do not reply to our message, My Lord," Commander Ken told the admiral, "and I believe they will not yield".

"So be it, Ken. Order the fleet to fire on those four ships and destroy them! Burn them into molten slag!" Lord Admiral Mentep stated firmly, a smile of victory growing upon his lips. He could almost taste victor now.

"Yes, Lord Admiral!" Commander Ken replied smartly.

However, before Ken could relay the order throughout the Vognar fleet, the four mysterious black airships shot out an astoundingly powerful blaze of bright white energy. It was a beam of terrific power. It was a great force of white fire that immediately blasted four of Lord Mentep's mighty airships out of the sky. The Vognar ships were blown to bits in horrendous explosions, they had been destroyed completely. The Vognars, officers and all Blues on the other ships of the Grand Fleet could not believe what they had just witnessed. Lord Mentep himself was momentarily astounded, confused, then angry.

"Sir," Commander Ken said to the Vognar admiral, "The enemy ships are... Well, they are now sending us a message asking about surrender."

"Hah! Of course they are! Now that they have attacked four of our ships they fear immediate and devastating reprisal. Well, we will not entertain any surrender now. Destroy them at once!" Lord Mentep ordered feeling a surge of anger and victory run through him now. The power of utter destruction was in his hands and he would use it.

"No, sir... ah...that is not exactly what they are asking," Commander Ken stated quite nervously now. He took a deep breathe and stated carefully, "The enemy ships are not asking for terms for *their* surrender, sir—they are asking for *our* surrender."

"*Our* surrender!" Lord Admiral Mentep barked in rage. "How dare they! Who do they think they are! I'll show them surrender! I'll show them utter destruction and death! Fire! All ships fire! *Fire and keep firing! Destroy them all!"*

All the Vognar ships fired their beam weapons, and it was a brutal and massive crescendo of torrential power, but after it was all done it hardly seemed to have any effect upon the four mysterious black airships that still hovered before the Vognar fleet apparently undamaged. It was almost as if they were now taunting the Vognar fleet.

Then—in the sudden blink of an eye—the four mysterious black ships disappeared.

They just blinked out of space and were gone.

There was utter silence, astounded wonder and consternation in the control rooms of each of the Vognar warships as if their commanders were trying to understand just what had happened. Suddenly the Vognars on every ship in the fleet cheered at what they saw as the defeat of the four opposing vessels.

"I believe they have been destroyed, all have exploded somehow," Commander Ken stated hopefully, though he could not figure out how it had happened. There had been no explosions, but there seemed no other explanation for what they had seen. "It appears you have won a great victory, My Lord."

Lord Mentep grunted acknowledgement, but remained skeptical about the results. Something did not seem right about this. Of course his own vessels had the power of invisibility, but he had not used it in this tiny battle, it hardly seemed necessary or worth the effort. It was also not a good tactic to let knowledge of his tricks be known to the enemy so soon. So he had not gone invisible—but had the four enemy ships somehow gone invisible? It seemed impossible. He was nervous by the way this battle had gone—and even though he had apparently destroyed the enemy ships—he had lost four good ships of his own to do so. The Vognar lord still wondered where these strange vessels were from? They were not Vognar vessels, of that the admiral was certain, and the green people from this eastern continent were not capable at all of such scientific feats, except perhaps…

Lord Mentep whispered a dire phrase of fear, "It must be the mysterious Kevans!"

"Kevans?" Commander Ken replied skeptically. "I have heard of them but they are just a rumor to scare children. They do not really exist."

"Have all vessels go to complete invisibility at once!" Lord Admiral Mentep ordered sharply. "I do not think these intruder vessels are dead yet."

Immediately more than ninety mighty warships of the Vognar Grand Fleet disappeared within the blink of an eye. They were gone.

Invisible.

"You think the four black ships are not dead?" Commander Ken asked his admiral. "Or, could it be… do they have the power of invisibility too?"

"We will find that out soon enough, commander," Admiral Mentep warned.

Ken saluted smartly and set about the tasks ordered.

Moments later a sudden and fierce fire rained down upon every warship in the Vognar fleet. It was white fire, intense and all consuming. It was devastating.

"So they have the invisibility power as well!" Admiral Mentep shouted, fearful, now realizing that while he had the odds in his favor—he was concerned now because his pilots told him they could not find the location of the four enemy vessels. They could not track the four black ships at all—even as it appeared that the enemy vessels could somehow track his own ships quite easily. The Vognar fleet was being hit hard now. Their mighty airships were exploding, burning, crashing down to the ground in crimson flames.

"This can not be happening!" Lord Admiral Mentep whispered in fear.

"No, My Lord!" Commander Ken responded, awaiting orders.

"Fire! Kill them all!" Lord Mentep barked order after order now. "Do not give up! All ships keep firing all weapons!"

Every Vognar airship fired all their weapons—at what they had no idea—for they could see no target—but the commanders had their orders. A deadly battle now raged between the invisible Vognar fleet and the invisible four black ships from Keva, but try as they might, the Vognars could not locate the invisible Kevan enemy. They could not hit the swiftly moving Kevan ships, even as more and more of their own airships went down one by one to defeat in devastating explosions. Lord Mentep soon realized that unless a change of tactics was made there could be but one outcome to this battle. Defeat! Such an outcome was unthinkable.

That was when Lord Admiral Mentep let out a dark curse and reluctantly barked an order throughout his fleet for a hasty regroup. It was a regroup, but it was in fact a retreat. It was an effort to save what was left of his fleet. The four black Kevan airships pursued the Vognar vessels relentlessly. They would not allow them to withdraw. The battle did not end but raged on for hours. Mentap finally ordered his remaining ships to break formation and split up—each commander was now on his own. They were ordered to scatter to the four winds. It did no good either. By the time that order was given it was too late.

By the end of the afternoon the last Vognar airship was blown out of the sky. Lord Admiral Mentep's own massive flagship burst forth in a dazzling explosion of blinding white beam radiance. Soon all the Vognar airships were destroyed. The Blue fleet ceased to exist. There were no survivors. Now finally, any attempt at Vognar conquest of the eastern continent of Ares was ended.

* * * *

When King Shamar of Keva arrived in the city of Lanar upon his secret mission for the Old Ones, he discovered that the city, indeed this entire province on the western continent of Vognar, was in utter turmoil and rebellion. The Vognar masters who ruled here over the Blue Lanar people had already been killed while an army of Lanar rebels was already formed under a new leader named Konor, who were all ready to march west upon the capital city of Vognar. They were ready to take down Okvon, and all who stood with the man they called not the Supreme Leader, but the 'Supreme Tyrant.'

Late in the day there were seen four mysterious black airships that stationed themselves in the sky above Lanar. They had arrived fresh from their victory over Lord Mentep's Grand Fleet, after which they had landed Emperor Jon Kirk and his men at Tarcos. Now the four black ships were here in the west. When they landed Shamar and Aron The Eldest loaded eager Lanar Blue warriors onboard and then they raced to the capital city of the Vognars to pay a visit to the Supreme Tyrant, Okvon. The quick small black ships made the trip across the wild western continent in just an hour.

As the four Kevan airships approached the outskirts of the Vognar capital city, their great victory over Mentep's fleet fresh in their minds, they debarked Konor and hundreds of troops comprised of vengeful Lanar Blues who were eager to continue to pursue the war on the ground in the capitol of their oppressors. Once that was accomplished the four black Kevan airships lifted off to fly overhead working together to destroy any of the city defenses that opposed the Lanar rebels.

The future history texts of Ares would tell of how the biggest mistake Lord Mentep and the mighty Grand Fleet of the Vognars had ever made was that they decided to meet four mysterious black airships in battle.

CHAPTER 17
VICTORY

Once the mysterious four black Kevan airships had defeated the Vognar Grand Fleet of Lord Mentep it had been easy for them to realize that not only was the battle theirs, but also the war. It would all be over soon and victory was at hand.

After the Vognar fleet was destroyed, and while Aron and Shamar turned their force to Lanar, they were victorious there and eventually left the Lanars to their own devices to take back their lands. Then they moved on to attack the Vognar capital city and fought another mad fight with the Vognar Home Fleet. That battle lasted almost one hour. Invisible ships against invisible ships, with the Vognars once again unable to locate the four Kevan ships. All of the ships of the Vognar home fleet were blown out of the sky. Not one survived.

The Lanar rebels under Konor took control of the city of Vognar and The Supreme Leader, Okvon, was put to the sword. The Kevan ships had no loses. Victory had been total and complete. So it was with much joy and elation that Aron and Shamar and their comrades set their four airships on a course back home to Keva.

The flight was rapid in the new swift airships. They were fast. However, once the four airships returned to Keva, Shamar and Aron were devastated by what they found and each man aboard the four vessels cried out in pain and horror. What they found was that instead of the small hidden city-state that had been their safe home for centuries, there was now only a huge empty black crater. They were shocked and stunned by what they saw. They could not comprehend it. Their pain, the dead, the incredible death and destruction was terrible. How had this happened?

The four airships approached the ruined city preparing to land to search for survivors, when they were suddenly attacked by a lone invisible Vognar airship that had been hiding in the hills beyond the city. The airship was the last survivor of Lord Mentep's vast armada that had somehow escaped the massive battle earlier. Somehow this ship had discovered Keva, probably because with Aron and all the Old Ones absent, the city was vulnerable, being unguarded for the first time in history. Now it was open to discovery. The attack on Keva had been a complete surprise and the lone Vognar airship had destroyed the helpless city and killed most of its people. It was a disaster of an unprecedented scope.

Shamar, Aron, and the Kevans immediately made their four airships go invisible and raced through the sky to fight back against the enemy vessel. Once invisible, the Vognar ship could not locate the Kevan ships and it was a quick matter for the Kevans to locate the Vognar vessel and blow it out of the sky with a blazing white beam of light that burned it to utter destruction. However, the quick and utter destruction of that last Vognar warship was of little consequence to the remaining grieving people of Keva. It was of little matter, save for revenge. Sometimes revenge was necessary—sometimes justice was revenge. All that did not matter much now either, for Keva was destroyed and most of its people were dead.

Shamar realized with shame that it was this one ship that had somehow escaped the Grand Fleet's defeat, it had somehow discovered the location of secret Keva. A secret no longer. A city no longer. Even now that every Vognar ship had been blown out of the sky, and every one of the Vogars was dead, it was all of small consequence to Shamar and Aron and the remaining Kevans. Shamar was devastated with the realization that he was now the king of a city-state that no longer existed. Aron The Eldest was leader of the Old Ones, a Great Council of wise elders for a nation of people who would probably some day become extinct. Keva was no more and the Kevan people were few, but under Shamar and Aron they vowed to rebuild their city and to repopulate their nation.

But first they had to bury the dead.

* * * *

With the Vognar fleet of Lord Mentep destroyed, the only thing left now for Zaor and I to do was to capture or exterminate the last few remnants of the Winged-men who had begun this war.

I gave the order to round up any remaining Zarans who quickly surrendered to my men and accepted terms of peace. They pledged to join with the green peoples in peace—or be exterminated. Some of the winged enemy with their old hatreds took the later choice, and they were quickly accommodated and dispatched. Mercy in this war was neither asked for, nor given. However, many of the younger winged creatures accepted the new world they now found themselves living in. After all, they did want to live. So they were allowed life but under strict observation and rules. They had to give up all their weapons, and their wings were bound so they could not fly unless we allowed them to do so. They could not mate and were only allowed to live on special guarded lands. In effect, reservations, but I did not worry about the implications of that now.

The important thing today was that the threat of the Winged-men of Zar was gone from Ares and the green race was free. Just as important, the Blue Vognar threat was apparently ended as well, the new regime on the western continent under Konor was peaceful and were now our allies. There still remained the great task of rebuilding and reconsolidating the Green Empire, and that had to begin soon. For I knew I had an even more enormous task ahead of me for the future. A far more imposing challenge.

That was the planet Zar!

It was eventually agreed that a small section in the north of the continent of Cos would be reserved for the Zarans who would now change their ways and that this settlement would be held under the tight control by a special governor appointed by myself and answerable to me personally. That seemed to end the winged menace on Ares once and for all and now all the green people could be finally safe and secure.

Now that the major part of the fighting was over, my lovely Sirah and I were now able to finally be together again, happily reunited and in each others arms. We had always held the hope of being reunited but now we were joyful that our dream had been granted and the future finally looked brighter.

In fact, Sirah told me with a mysterious smile, there was another of our dreams that had also been granted.

"What do you mean?" I asked curiously. I looked her in the eyes a bit suspicious when I saw the smile playing across her lips, so I knew that she was apparently bursting with joy to tell me something special. I could not think of what it might be.

"My Emperor, my love, I have news," she said with a wide smile, then she added simply, "I am with child."

I looked at her in shock, truly stunned, but absolutely delighted, overawed all at once. I quickly kissed her and hugged her and held her tightly to me—but not *too* tightly—and then I asked her a million questions.

Sirah only smiled and laughed, "The birthing will not be for some time, Jon Kirk, and I do not know if the child will be male or female."

"What does it matter!" I cried, delighted. I was going to be a father! I looked at Sirah lovingly, "You have made me so happy!"

"What shall we name him—or her?" Sirah asked me laughing happily.

I smiled, "We have time, my love, you make the choice, whatever makes you happy."

"We will choose together, my husband. When the time comes."

I nodded, "Ah, now…when will that be? Roughly." I asked blown over by the wonderful news but overjoyed.

"One hundred days should be the time of the birthing. Though one can never expect an exact time in these matters. The Spirit of Life works on it's own schedule."

"Of course." I sighed. "One hundred days from now, it can not come soon enough."

"Nor for me, my love. But in the meantime you have your Emperor duties to fulfill, so get to work, there is much for you to do!"

"Yes, My Empress," I said with a smile and a light bow at her order. I knew she was right.

All the people of Tarcos cheered when I, Jon Kirk, Emperor of the Green Empire as it was now called, and my friend General Zaor, returned to them. The celebrations rang throughout the city and all the green lands and all other cities upon Ares. The green peoples were free and safe, and the dreaded flying enemy had been defeated once and for all.

Or so I hoped. Even so, I knew there was one more battle yet to fight and win.

Over the next weeks my duties weighed heavily upon my mind, especially now with a child on the way. There was much work that had to be done. Primarily among that work was to discover the location of the secret city-state of Keva. There had been no news from the Kevans since the defeat of the Zarans and Vognars.

I felt it was my duty as Emperor to find Keva and visit King Shamar, and Aron The Eldest and the other Old Ones of that mysterious secret city to make some kind of treaty or alliance. I knew we could not neglect this tiny, but powerful, city-state, but we did not know their secret location. It was the mind powers of the Old Ones of Keva that had saved the struggling humans of the Green Empire. So I knew we must seek them out. We owed them much. I also realized we needed their aid in the battle to come.

However, no matter how hard I had my warriors and scouts look, no matter how many scouts and expeditions we sent to explore, Keva was not to be found. In fact, I heard no word, nor any message from King Shamar or Aron The Eldest ever again. I knew they were out there somewhere certainly, and they were friends and potential allies, but those of Keva remained as they always have been—alone, separate and aloof from all other Greens. It was their way. It was their custom. Secrecy was how the tiny city of Keva had remained free for so long. I realized the small city was in some ways analogous to the Switzerland of my own home world. They did not want to be contacted, they remain aloof from all others and wanted to be left alone. They did not like to be involved in the affairs of men. I knew I would eventually respect their wishes, but for now I had to find the city and talk to their leaders. Perhaps some day the scouts would no longer go forth, and the expeditions would be called back home to Tarcos, and the location of Keva would remain secret. But not for some while. Not until I had spoken with Shamar and Aron The Eldest one more time about the future.

So while I sent out expedition after expedition in search of the Kevans, they came back with nothing to report. I eventually sent Sahn Jor in one of our newly captured airships to far away Vognar on a secret mission—to the western continent on the other side of the planet Ares. Sahn Jor was sent to seek out any news of the Kevans from the new Vognar government and to scout the more lonely places on that land where a hidden city might be secreted.

Konor, the new Blue military leader of Lanar was helpful. He told us he wanted to end the war and barbarism promulgated under

Okvon's tyranny. The new country he created was for Blues and Greens living together in peace. It was free and the people were far better off with Konor as ruler. He said the entire Vognar air fleet had been destroyed in the war. They did not know how it had been done other than by four mysterious black ships—I did not mention anything about the people of Keva or their powers to him. The remaining Blues had no news of their lost airships or Grand Fleet, and not one vessel had ever returned from the invasion. There had been no survivors. So nothing was known. It seemed finding out anything from the Blues about the location of Keva would only lead to a dead end.

After a month of searching, Sahn Jor returned to Tarcos, much weary for his efforts without any definite information on the whereabouts of the mysterious Kevans and their secret city. It was as if the entire city had just disappeared and he wondered if in fact it had been destroyed, wiped off the face of the planet somehow. Of course, Sahn Jor did not know for certain this had actually happened, but he felt there could be no other alternative and that is what he reported to me. His words proved to be prophetic.

"There is a new nation that rules on the vast continent of Vognar now," Sahn Jor told me, upon his return to Tarcos. "It is now called the Kingdom of Lanar. Konor has been proclaimed the king there. He is a good man. The Blues and Greens live together in peace for the first time. They are all better off. They are our allies now, Okvon and his few supporters have been executed."

"So Konor told me on my last visit," I replied casually. "What of Keva?"

Sahn Jor nodded, then continued, "The Lanars have told me of the rebellion and battles that took place against the old regime of Okvon and the death struggle between the Lanars and Vognars on the western continent of Ares. Many of the Blues were killed in the war, many more remain and support Konor."

I nodded, impatiently, "What about Keva?"

Shan Jor looked at me closely, "The Kevans are a different matter, that city seems to be no more. I fear it was somehow destroyed. While no one mourns the passing of Okvon and the hated Vognars under his rule, the people there are doing well now. I searched for Keva, but without any luck. Apparently it was a quick death for our friends from Keva in their secret city here on this continent. I found some ruins, it was utter devastation. A Vognar ship seems to have slipped away from the main battle and found the city. No one in the city during could have survived their attack. I found graves though, so someone had to have dug them. So someone from Keva is still alive. However, there are no people living there now. Any survivors have left. Wherever they have gone—I can not guess. I could find no information on them relocating upon the western continent other than rumors, but that seems enough, for it is most like them to not want to be found, so I am not surprised. They are a most unsocial people. There extinction is very sad."

"I do not believe they are extinct," I said firmly, hope filling a large empty space in my heart for the people of Keva.

Sahn Jor looked at me closely and said, "It is hard for me to believe that Shamar and Aron The Eldest of the Old Ones, and all those others from Keva are dead and gone. Our world is truly empty without them"

"It is a great tragedy, and a terrible loss that all their great wisdom and mind powers may be lost to us forever," I said softly, thinking of my friend Shamar and wondering what had happened to him. Had he fallen in battle? Where was he? And what had befallen Aron The Eldest and all the others? I felt a keen kinship with them all.

Shan Jor looked at me carefully and offered a thoughtful look, "The names Shamar and Aron still ring true in the voices of those who live in the West, Jon Kirk. I have heard these names spoken in some unusual places. In the new Kingdom of Lanar I heard rumor of a small northern place called Kev. A tiny speck really, secret and hidden, if in fact it truly exists at all. All deny it does exist. One of the princes there is of interest to me, it is said he is called by the name of Samar, or could it be Shamar? I heard that the governor is said to be a wily old man by the name of Arlon… or is it perhaps Aron? They are a most reclusive people. Unsocial in the extreme. No one ever sees either of these men, nor any of these people thereabouts. It is almost as if they are invisible."

"They wish to be invisible," I said softly.

Sahn Jor nodded, continuing with his report, "Local people told me strange things about the people of Kev, but you know how these primitive country folk can be. Suspicious and prone to superstition. I could not gain a meeting with either of these men, nor would they reply to my messages or entreaties for me to be allowed entrance to their country. It is closed off, and the actual whereabouts of the village is a mystery. It may, in fact, be invisible, or even secreted underground. They are very strict about their privacy. It seems these two men, with a few families, might just be the last survivors of Keva. These noble people have now made themselves outcasts on their own world because of the great mind power they possess. These may be the last of the Kevans of whom I was to search, Jon Kirk, but they still remain hidden and inaccessible."

I nodded sadly. I knew the way those of Keva were.

"It appears they are gone," Zaor added in a sad tone. "They have escaped to a new life and I wish them well. Thank the gods they still live. Somewhere."

"Yes, those that have survived are lucky, as are we all," I stated as I put my arm around my Empress, the lovely Lady Sirah. I held her tightly and she held me closely bringing her lips up to my own.

"I never want us to be separated ever again, my love," Sirah told me as we kissed with heated passion. Then she smiled and said, "Thank you, my love—My Emperor—for all you have done for me, and for my people."

I softly hugged my wife close to me. I kissed her lips and replied joyfully, "Thank you, my wife, and thank you for the little one growing inside you."

Sirah gave me a little smile and lightly patted her belly knowingly. Was it getting bigger already?

I sighed, keeping my mind on my mission. I looked at all those around and stated boldly, "There is much we have to do yet. Now we have an entire new civilization to build up from scratch and we have one more enemy to guard against. Grusus, Bron and their army while dead and defeated, did not originate from Ares. These winged-men were new troops brought in from the planet Zar to retake our world. That means our people are still in danger. We must be ready for the enemy to come again, for I am sure they will try once more to take back this world and enslave the green peoples."

"Then we will fight them again and win again!" Zaor growled defiantly.

"No," I stated firmly. "We have airships now. If they can be made to travel through space…?"

"I see," Zaor said approvingly. "I like it, but can it be done?"

"We shall see. If possible we will use the knowledge gained from the Vognar and Kevan flying ships, along with their invisibility device and beam weapons to take this war to the enemy home planet of Zar. Then we shall see how these Winged-men like being conquered!"

"Yes, Jon Kirk," Zaor stated firmly, "I do like your plan."

"What we do in life, shall echo through eternity!" I said with grim determination.

Zaor nodded with a wry smile, "What we do in life shall echo through eternity, Jon Kirk, and I shall pray for that day, my friend."

"I too will welcome that day, my love," Sirah added as she hugged me all the more tightly, then smothering my lips with warm loving kisses, she added in a low whisper, "As will our little one."

ABOUT THE AUTHOR

GARY LOVISI is a Brooklyn-based author and science fiction fan who was inspired early in life by the John Carter of Mars books—and all the great works of Edgar Rice Burroughs—which he first read as a teenager in the 1960s. In his Jon Kirk of Ares Chronicles, he seeks to capture the sense of wonder, rousing pulse-pounding action, and strange adventures on alien worlds, that made Burroughs' classic books so much fun to read. Lovisi has written in all genres of fiction, from short stories to novels; and non-fiction about authors, artists, and book collecting. He edits *Paperback Parade* magazine and founded Gryphon Books. He was short-listed for a Mystery Writers of America Edgar Award for the Best Short Story of the Year, and received a Spur Award from the Western Writers of America. Lovisi's first Jon Kirk of Ares novel, *The Winged-Men* was published by Wildside Press in 2014. Now with these two latest original novels in the series from Wildside Press: *The Invisible Men* (#2) and *The Space Men* (#3), the Jon Kirk of Ares Chronicles is off and running, with more original novels planned. To find out more about Lovisi, his writing, other books, or Jon Kirk of Ares Chronicles news, check his website: www.gryphonbooks.com.

ABOUT THE COVER ARTIST

MARCUS BOAS is a New York City illustrator, and a master of vivid fantasy and science fiction art. His use of striking colors and heroic images in his art dazzles all who view it. His stunning work has been a mainstay used on the covers of many books and magazines in the fantasy field over his decades long art career. A big fan of Edgar Rice Burroughs, and especially the John Carter of Mars series, Marcus is a natural to do the covers for the Jon Kirk of Ares Chronicles. You can see some of his outstanding work collected in such books as *Heroic Fantasy*, *Jungle*, and others published by Kaso Comics at www.kasocomics.com. Wonderful prints are also available for some of his most beautiful work.

ABOUT THE MAPMAKER

LUCILLE CALI is a Brooklyn, New York free-lance artist whose map of Ares is based upon the original map first drawn by the author in 1971, when he wrote the first book in the Jon Kirk of Ares Chronicles. Cali has done numerous covers for various Gryphon Books as well as issues of *Hardboiled* magazine and is a very versatile artist.

www.ingramcontent.com/pod-product-compliance
Lightning Source LLC
Chambersburg PA
CBHW020142180626
46810CB00004B/1684